"What the heck, Allie, let's get it over with," Connor growled.

And his mouth came down on hers before she could say another word.

Allie closed her eyes so that all she could feel were Connor's fingers closed warm and firm over her knuckles, and his mouth softly tasting her. His mouth was firm, warm, smooth. His long lashes tickled her cheeks as he broke contact for just an instant and moved his head to the side. Allie's bottom lip trembled and dropped open as she let out a slow gasp.

Allie was overwhelmed by the power of Connor's kiss. Because the kiss had taken control of both of them, had acquired a life of its own. The kiss mattered. It was the crystallization of everything she had begun to feel about him. A trust and a connection deeper than she'd have thought possible in so short a time. A sense of promise, as if the kiss was only the beginning....

Dear Reader,

As Silhouette's yearlong anniversary celebration continues, Romance again delivers six unique stories about the poignant journey from courtship to commitment.

Teresa Southwick invites you back to STORKVILLE, USA, where a wealthy playboy has the gossips stumped with his latest transaction: *The Acquired Bride*…and her triplet kids! *New York Times* bestselling author Kasey Michaels contributes the second title in THE CHANDLERS REQUEST… miniseries, *Jessie's Expecting*. Judy Christenberry spins off her popular THE CIRCLE K SISTERS with a story involving a blizzard, a roadside motel with one bed left, a gorgeous, honor-bound rancher…and his *Snowbound Sweetheart*.

New from Donna Clayton is SINGLE DOCTOR DADS! In the premiere story of this wonderful series, a first-time father strikes *The Nanny Proposal* with a woman whose timely hiring quickly proves less serendipitous and more carefully, *lovingly*, staged…. Lilian Darcy pens yet another edgy, uplifting story with *Raising Baby Jane*. And debut author Jackie Braun delivers pure romantic fantasy as a down-on-her-luck waitress receives an intriguing order from the man of her dreams: *One Fiancée To Go, Please*.

Next month, look for the exciting finales of STORKVILLE, USA and THE CHANDLERS REQUEST… And the wait is over as Carolyn Zane's BRUBAKER BRIDES make their grand reappearance!

Happy Reading!

Mary-Theresa Hussey

Mary-Theresa Hussey
Senior Editor

Please address questions and book requests to:
Silhouette Reader Service
U.S.: 3010 Walden Ave., P.O. Box 1325, Buffalo, NY 14269
Canadian: P.O. Box 609, Fort Erie, Ont. L2A 5X3

Raising Baby Jane

LILIAN DARCY

SILHOUETTE *Romance*

Published by Silhouette Books

America's Publisher of Contemporary Romance

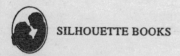 SILHOUETTE BOOKS

ISBN 0-373-19478-1

RAISING BABY JANE

Copyright © 2000 by Lilian Darcy

This edition published by arrangement with Harlequin Books S.A.

Visit Silhouette at www.eHarlequin.com

Printed in U.S.A.

Books by Lilian Darcy

Silhouette Romance

The Baby Bond #1390
Her Sister's Child #1449
Raising Baby Jane #1478

LILIAN DARCY

Since her marriage to an irresistible New Yorker over ten years ago, Lilian Darcy has divided her time between various parts of the United States and her native Australia. Her children hold dual citizenship, and in her writing she tries to embody the shared strength of the two cultures—heroism, warmth and down-to-earth values. Although new to Silhouette, she has written over thirty books for the Harlequin Mills & Boon Medical Romance line and is now looking forward to creating strong, passionate stories for a whole new set of readers.

IT'S OUR 20th ANNIVERSARY!
We'll be celebrating all year,
Continuing with these fabulous titles,
On sale in October 2000.

Desire

#1321 The Dakota Man
Joan Hohl

#1322 Rancher's Proposition
Anne Marie Winston

#1323 First Comes Love
Elizabeth Bevarly

#1324 Fortune's Secret Child
Shawna Delacorte

#1325 Marooned With a Marine
Maureen Child

#1326 Baby: MacAllister-Made
Joan Elliott Pickart

Romance

#1474 The Acquired Bride
Teresa Southwick

#1475 Jessie's Expecting
Kasey Michaels

#1476 Snowbound Sweetheart
Judy Christenberry

#1477 The Nanny Proposal
Donna Clayton

#1478 Raising Baby Jane
Lilian Darcy

#1479 One Fiancée To Go, Please
Jackie Braun

Special Edition

#1351 Bachelor's Baby Promise
Barbara McMahon

#1352 Marrying a Delacourt
Sherryl Woods

#1353 Millionaire Takes a Bride
Pamela Toth

#1354 A Bundle of Miracles
Amy Frazier

#1355 Hidden in a Heartbeat
Patricia McLinn

#1356 Stranger in a Small Town
Ann Roth

Intimate Moments

#1033 Who Do You Love?
Maggie Shayne/
Marilyn Pappano

#1034 Her Secret Weapon
Beverly Barton

#1035 A Thanksgiving to Remember
Margaret Watson

#1036 The Return of Luke McGuire
Justine Davis

#1037 The Lawman Meets His Bride
Meagan McKinney

#1038 The Virgin Beauty
Claire King

Chapter One

"Just remind me one more time why I agreed to do this!" Allie Todd growled at her sister Karen Pirelli.

Karen didn't answer. She was gripping the steering wheel of the minivan so hard that her knuckles were white. Her shoulders were hunched, her forehead was pleated and those little sounds coming from her mouth were probably prayers.

The road—track—they were driving on probably wouldn't have been in great shape even on a dry summer's day. At the end of a brief January thaw, after several big snowstorms already this winter, it was slushy and slippery and positively frightening.

"Can't be much farther," Karen muttered, peering ahead. "Connor said—"

She broke off. They'd come out of the dark pine woods into a cleared space that in summer would have had room for several cars. It must have been plowed a couple of times this winter. There was dirty snow heaped up in lumpy, untidy banks on two sides. But it hadn't been plowed recently.

On the third side, there was the track that Karen had just negotiated, and on the fourth—

Karen slammed on the brakes. Worst thing you could do on a snow-slippery road. Allie could have told her that, though if she'd been driving herself, she would probably have panicked, as Karen had, and made the same mistake.

The minivan suddenly embarked on a skating career. It swirled elegantly in one direction then the other, before it came finally to a stop about two inches from the sharp, four-foot drop down to the sheet of lake ice.

Karen told Allie shakily, "I owe you one, okay?"

But Allie shook her head. "No. That's one thing you'll *never* have to say to me, Karen. You know that." She cleared her throat to get rid of the sudden huskiness in her voice, then added, "I shouldn't have complained about coming up here."

"No," Karen argued, "*I* shouldn't have asked you to do this, when I know it's so hard for you to—" She changed tack quickly. "And anyway, I know you're not much of a cabin gal."

"Just how primitive is it going to be, did he happen to say?"

"No, he didn't."

They both sat in the front of the minivan, peering out across the white lake to the snow-covered island in the distance.

Karen slumped her arms onto the steering wheel and groaned, still looking sick.

"Are you okay?" Allie demanded uselessly.

"I'm fine." She took a shaky breath. Then she took another one. "I meant to tell you on the way up, but you were sleeping. I've got some news. I— I'm pregnant, Allie."

"Oh, Karen, that's wonderful! That's just so great!" Allie said, her voice fogging again.

"I know." Karen smiled, relief evident in her face. Allie understood at once that her sister hadn't been confident about how she'd receive the news. "John and I are just so thrilled," she went on. "Although I feel pretty disgusting a lot of the time, and—"

She stopped, and they both turned instinctively to look at the six-month-old baby asleep in the backseat. She was a beautiful girl. Just beautiful. On her head there was a fine growth of silky, dark-gold hair. On her plump rosy cheeks, there were two fans of extraordinarily long, satiny black lashes. Her skin was so peachy and translucent that a blue vein across her nose showed quite clearly. It was the prettiest, purest color.

There was a short silence, then Allie carefully voiced a small part of what they were both thinking. "They'll be very close in age."

"I know. Thirteen months apart."

"Jane won't remember..." Allie began.

"...what it was like before she had a baby brother or sister," Karen finished. "Don't worry about it, Allie, it's not a problem. Really! John and I have been wanting a big family for so long. There were so many times we despaired that it would ever happen. And you know that nothing about what we're doing with this is a problem for me. Whatever you decide about anything in the future, if you want—''

''It's okay, Karen,'' Allie answered with difficulty. ''I know. You've promised me that from the beginning. I guess I'm still working things out.''

''It's only that my energy levels are down at the moment. John's away on business till Wednesday. I should have gone with him, taken a break, but the chance to do this book cover was too good to turn down. The movie rights for it have already been sold. Nancy Sherlock is *huge* these days.''

''And with a temperament to match, evidently.''

''With a temperament to ma—'' Karen began to agree. Then she stopped abruptly and put her hand over her mouth, gripped by nausea.

''Let's get you out of this car, so you can walk around and get some air.''

''I can't open the door.''

''I know. And I'm not letting you climb across to my side in your condition. Not with that big old gearshift in the way.''

Allie quickly jammed on her dark blue velour hat and wriggled her fingers into warm woolly gloves, then jumped out of the car and went round to the driver's side. ''Hang in there,'' she ordered her sister, both protective and stern. ''I'm going to shovel back the snow as quick as I can. You still look like you're about to throw up.''

''Might,'' Karen agreed through clenched teeth.

She folded her arms across the steering wheel and buried her face in them, breathing carefully.

Not caring that her gloves were immediately soaked through, Allie began to drag armfuls of snow out of the way of the door. It was slower work than she'd anticipated. The snow bank was like a big, puffy quilt, and the van looked as if it had decided to snuggle in for the night.

"Would a shovel help?" said a male voice.

Allie looked up, startled, and found the orange scoop of a snow shovel staring her in the face. She sat back on her haunches, a little breathless and hot, and looked up higher. A handle. A leather-gloved hand. A big, thick, black coat sleeve ending in an impressive shoulder. Finally, a man's face beneath a black, stretchy wool hat. He had the bluest eyes she'd ever seen.

There was something about him that immediately had Allie off balance. Literally. She stumbled and wasn't steady as she straightened. It didn't help that she hadn't heard his approach across the slightly softened ice, above the effortful pant of her breathing and the sound of scraping snow.

Karen still had her head hidden in her arms, but she had heard his voice.

"Connor?" came her muffled query.

"Yeah, hi." He leaned an arm on the minivan's door frame and examined Karen through the half-open window. "I guess you didn't intend on parking quite so close to the lake, right?"

"Right."

"Feeling sick?"

"Right again."

"Yeah, it can shake you up, a near miss like that. That drop's pretty sharp."

"Connor, this is Allie. Allie, meet Connor Callahan. Sorry...about the...informality." She lapsed into silence once more and went on taking those deep, careful breaths.

"Nice to meet you, Allie."

Connor stuck out his glove and she shook it, then saw his face as the action squeezed a trickle of icy water from the sodden wool. His grimace was designed to get a reaction from her, and it worked.

She laughed. "Not exactly waterproof, I'm afraid."

Without another word, only a speaking glance, he began to shovel back the snow from the door. He moved with an efficiency that looked effortless, and he was singing what seemed to be a sea shanty under his breath. It was a very appealing sound and Allie almost felt like joining in.

"You've done this before, haven't you?" she suggested after a moment.

"Yeah, and I'm sorry I didn't get to do it before you got here," he said. "Some stuff came up at work that I had to deal with before I could take off. I'd hoped to get here a couple of hours earlier, and I should have told Karen to pack some snow chains."

"Nice idea," Allie agreed easily, "assuming either of us knew how to put them on."

She peeled off the sopping gloves, dropped them onto the roof of the minivan with a gesture of distaste and tucked her hands beneath her upper arms to warm them.

Connor straightened from his work for a moment and studied her thoughtfully.

She was petite, a compact bundle of dark blue with her arms folded like that. She was smaller than her sister, and darker, too. Hair of a glossy black-brown escaped from beneath her hat and reached her shoulders.

He couldn't see much of her face. She had that velour hat jammed down so low, it shaded her eyes completely. All he could see was a soft mouth, not wide but gorgeously shaped, and high, well-defined cheeks that were pink from the cold. She would have looked about sixteen if there hadn't been such a determined, contained aura to her pose and her expression.

He'd never been slow to form first impressions about a woman. With this one, those impressions were good. He had a feeling that the favor his pretty neighbor had pressed on him might turn out to be interesting.

Allie was hopping up and down now, trying to keep her feet warm. He hoped they weren't as wet as her gloves in those leather boots, meant for city streets.

"Your sister hasn't told me much about you," he said to her with a slow grin, "but I'm getting the impression you're not the wilderness type."

"Not since I quit Girl Scouts at age twelve," she agreed. "I'm a lot more the curling-up-in-front-of-a - blazing - fire - with - some - good - music - and - a - book - and - a - mug - of - hot - chocolate type. Is...uh... that going to be a problem this weekend?''

Allie asked the question a little nervously. Her boots were leaking and her hands were throbbing. She really didn't want to hear that this cabin they were headed for had no electricity and one smoky woodstove in a ramshackle kitchen.

"You mean does my brother's place have a blazing fire?" Connor asked.

"For starters, yes."

"I can arrange it," he drawled.

He had a jaw as square and strong as his snow shovel, a body like a professional sportsman and a voice like gravel dripping with melted fudge. Allie resisted the impulse to conclude that the man could probably "arrange" just about anything he wanted. In the nicest possible way.

As he returned to work, she had to fight the urge to say to him, "Sing that sea shanty again," because the rhythm of it had meshed so well with the rhythm of his body, and he had the growling, rollicking singing voice of a pirate.

"Okay, Karen, that's freed it now," he said, after a couple more minutes. "Why don't you get out and I'll move the car to a safer spot?"

"Thanks," Karen answered, straightening at last from the steering wheel where she'd been resting her head on her arms.

She climbed awkwardly out onto the snow, and the fresh, cold air brought some healthy color back into her cheeks.

Connor slid into the driver's seat, turned the ignition and maneuvered the minivan so that it sat neatly beside his own Range Rover. While he was doing so, Allie said quietly to her sister, "Going to be okay?"

"Fine now," Karen nodded.

"Does he know about the baby?"

"Not yet. We've only just started telling family. You're the first apart from Mom and Dad and John's parents."

"I won't say anything this weekend, then."

"I may have to tell him, if I keep getting sick like this. I guess I'm nervous about that book cover, which isn't helping. Nancy Sherlock has already rejected two previous versions done by other artists, and they must have roped me in as a desperation measure. I've never done cover art for an author this big before. Apparently, she wants a 'natural feel.' She thought the backdrop and the models they used before were 'too fake.' And she saw the covers I did for Gloria Blackmore's 'Harvest' trilogy and loved them."

"So there you are," Allie soothed. "She loves your stuff."

Karen made a face. "She has a reputation for changing her mind without warning. I mean, was she serious about those models? I decided to try it with you guys because you're both photogenic, but you're not professionals. Only maybe that was crazy?"

"Trust your intuition, Karen," Allie soothed

again. "You'll calm down once you get behind your camera."

"Which reminds me, I'd like to get some photos of the lake right now before the light changes. There's a great feel and quality to it at the moment, so crisp and clean. And before Janey wakes up."

Allie nodded, ignoring the slight tightening of her throat that happened every time her sister mentioned baby Jane, especially in that tender yet casual way.

Connor was with them again, and had heard Karen's words. "Having an attack of inspiration?"

"If that suits you," Karen nodded. She was already on her way to the rear door of the van to get out her camera equipment.

"It's fine," he agreed. "I'll bring the snowmobile across for our gear. I checked the ice, and it's rock-solid out there. The softening from the thaw is only in the top half inch. Meanwhile, my fellow 'model' here, can look after her little niece if she wakes up."

He tossed a casual grin across to Allie, then his face darkened and fell, and she knew she hadn't managed to hide her stricken expression. Suddenly, she realized how vulnerable she was going to be this weekend, having to spend it so close to Karen and Jane with a stranger looking on.

"Hey," Connor came in quickly, "Did I scare you? I didn't mean to. You're not nervous about this gig, surely? Treat it as a joke. *I* am! I've never modeled for anything before."

"Neither have I," she managed.

"And the idea of having your sister do one of those vibrant, romantic book-cover paintings of hers based on photos of *us* tickles me to death. I leaped at the chance to goof off for a three-day weekend."

"I guess I should look at it that way, too," Allie replied, thankful that he'd unknowingly given her an easy way out of admitting what was really eating away at her heart.

"Or is it the thought of changing a diaper that's so frightening?" he teased.

Could he read her mind?

"Yes, it's terrifying," she answered, trying to make it sound like a joke. "I've never changed a diaper in my life."

"Seriously?"

"Seriously."

He raised one eyebrow and tucked in the corner of his mouth, and she could tell he wasn't impressed. Damn it, damn it, it was none of his business! Thrust deep in the pockets of her coat, her thawing hands were shaking.

"I'll be back in about five minutes," he said, then paused for a second. "No, make that ten. I have a couple of things to do inside the house."

"Ten minutes. Okay," she nodded.

Karen had her camera lens attached and her tripod positioned out on the wooden boat dock that thrust out into the lake from the far end of the parking lot. Jane was still fast asleep in her car seat. The engine was switched off now, so the car's heating wasn't on anymore. She'd get cold, soon.

Opening the door of the minivan as soundlessly as she could, Allie reached in and unfolded the baby quilt that was sitting on top of the diaper bag. She

tucked it in around Jane as well as she could with
the restraining bar of the baby seat in the way, hard-
ening herself against any ambush of tenderness. Had
Karen's news about her pregnancy changed anything? The possibility overwhelmed her.

Then she closed up the car again, leaving one
window open just a crack to let in some air, and
went over to her sister.

"Have you known him long?" It was almost an
accusation.

Karen looked up from her viewfinder. "Nearly
five months," she said, betraying no surprise at the
question. "Maybe you don't remember. His place
used to be rented out, then it came up for sale and
was empty for about three months until he bought
it. He moved in early September, and that was when
we first met him."

Allie nodded. The explanation told her everything
she wanted to know. But Karen had more to say.

"He's a great guy, Allie. The kind you could trust
with your life. John and I have met his parents and
two of his brothers, and they're a close, wonderful
family."

"That's good to know," Allie answered. She
trusted her sister's judgment in a way that she
trusted few other things in life these days. Then,
changing the subject deliberately, she added, "Getting some good stuff?"

"Don't know yet," Karen answered. Her eye was
already back peering through the viewfinder. "But
I'm not taking any chances on this. I'm going to
shoot as much film as I can so that there's no way

Nancy can come up with a suggestion for a scene that I can't cover. I love those clouds just feathering above the mountains." She waved a hand. "I want to take a whole lot of winter-landscape shots as well, for this photographic kids' book I'm planning on the four seasons."

Allie laughed. This was typical of Karen. She had energy to burn, and usually more irons in the fire, professionally and personally, than she could count. Allie repeated this gentle accusation out loud.

"Irons in the fire?" Karen looked up, with a self-conscious expression. "What do you mean?"

"Well, despite your being so nervous about the Nancy Sherlock cover, you still have time to think about a kids' book."

Karen's expression cleared. "Oh. Right. That."

"Why, what did you think I meant?"

"Nothing." Very offhand. Not looking at Allie. Very seriously taking pictures and talking about the book cover again.

Allie felt a tiny tickle of suspicion and alarm, but she let it slide.

"I'm going to do night shots, interiors," Karen was saying. "And I want to get out the clothing this afternoon, if we can, so I can get some shots of you wearing—"

She stopped abruptly and gave a hiss of dismay. She'd been taking pictures as she talked, changing lenses, moving the tripod, and the camera had just made a strangled, clicking sound that even Allie recognized wasn't right.

"Hang on," Karen said carefully, "Let's try

again." She pressed the camera's small silver button but nothing happened. "I'm not going to panic," she informed Allie in a panicky voice.

"Okay, good," Allie agreed.

"I'm just going to check out each possibility very carefully and slowly," she continued, madly rattling, clicking, shaking and winding every bit of delicate camera apparatus that she could lay her hands on.

"Sounds sensible."

"And if there *is* something wrong with it that I can't fix," she announced, ripping the entire roll of film out of the camera in several torn sections and dropping them onto the ice-encrusted dock, "I'm not going to overreact."

All of which didn't fully explain why Connor was greeted, on his return with the snowmobile several minutes later, with the news that as soon as baby Jane and all the bags were unloaded, he had to drive the minivan up to the main road. Karen needed to make an emergency dash into Albany to get her very expensive, state-of-the-art, obscure brand of camera repaired immediately.

"I'll be gone three hours max," she finished.

"Karen, it's over an hour's drive each way," Connor pointed out patiently. "And then you have to get the—"

"Okay, three and a half. But I'll be back before dark."

"It's already nearly four o'clock."

"Before dinner." She paused at last, and listened. "That's Jane waking up, Allie."

"Yes, I can hear her."

Jane was waking up happy. There were some singing and cooing and gurgling sounds coming from the backseat of the van.

"If you can get her and put on her snowsuit, Allie, then Connor can take you and her and the diaper bag over to the cabin now, while I unload the rest of our gear. Then he can come straight back and drive me up to the main road. I can be on my way in five minutes."

This time, Connor didn't even bother to offer a more realistic time-frame, and Allie was too busy thinking, *Jane. I'm going to have to look after Jane. All by myself. No one else around at all. For at least half an hour while Connor drives up and walks back down and loads our gear onto the snowmobile. And then when he gets back, it'll be just him and me and Jane. For hours. I don't want to do it. I'm scared. I'm not ready. I don't know yet if I'll ever be ready. Why can't Karen see that? Why isn't she helping me with this?*

Because Karen was scared, too.

Allie could see it and hear it in the panicky plans and the jittery movements. First and foremost, Karen was a mother and a wife. She wanted a big, loving, untidy family in her big Victorian house next to Connor's. But she had a strong creative drive as well.

Her career as a commercial artist and photographer was important to her, this cover for a guaranteed bestseller was her biggest break so far. She needed to continue this success if she and John were to afford that parcel of kids they dreamed of. She didn't want to blow it, and her camera had jammed, and of course she was scared.

"Sounds do-able," Connor said. He gave an apparently casual glance at the horizon over the snow-covered mountains that ringed Diamond Lake and added, half under his breath, "More or less. If we're lucky." Then aloud he said, "Let's go, Allie."

"Don't hold dinner for me," Karen told Connor. "Although I'll definitely be back."

"Of course you will," Connor soothed her, as if he hadn't just spent five minutes trying to convince her she shouldn't go in the first place. He hunched his shoulders against the growing chill. It was only just past four o'clock, but the day was darkening by the minute. There was bad weather in the forecast, although it hadn't made its appearance yet.

"And for Jane you'll need to—" She tucked a strand of light brown hair behind her ear and it stuck out messily, adding to her aura of nervous distraction.

"I know a fair bit about babies," Connor soothed her again.

"Allie...doesn't."

"I gathered that," he nodded.

He was actually a little put off by how cold Allie seemed toward her cute little niece. Maybe his positive first impressions were going to need some revision. She had neatly ducked the task of getting Jane into her snowsuit and Karen had done it instead, with a tight face. Was she angry at her sister's lack of interest?

I would be, Connor decided inwardly. *It doesn't take much to show a little warmth toward a baby.*

"Look after her—and Allie," Karen said now.

"Oh. Sure. Of course." Did Allie need looking after?

"Seriously, Connor." For a moment, Karen actually held still long enough to look him in the eye. "She's been through a really rough time, and she's such a great person. Warm, funny, sincere." She stopped suddenly, as if rethinking the wisdom of what she'd just said. "Anyway, I'll be back pretty soon. I know what you said about the forecast, but look at that sky." She waved in the direction where it was still blue. "Does that look like a storm to you?"

It didn't, and Connor didn't waste his breath pointing to the clouds that had begun to build behind them. She could well be right. The storm would pass to the west, or hold off altogether.

"And I have my cell phone," Karen was saying. "Oh, this is such a nightmare!"

"No, it isn't. Really, it isn't."

She hadn't heard. "See you later."

She was gone in a flurry of dirty roadside snow seconds later, and so he turned with a fatalistic shrug and began to walk back down the winding quarter mile of track to Diamond Lake.

Allie stood outside to greet him after he'd brought the snowmobile across the lake and wheeled it around to park it by the front door.

"You said this place was a cabin," she said accusingly.

"Never did," he returned lightly, following her inside. She peeled off her coat to reveal black pants tucked into damp leather boots, and a pale blue angora sweater that hugged her small frame.

He decided Allie was an assertive woman, despite her size! If he hadn't heard it in her voice, he'd have seen it in the lift of her strong, but graceful jaw and in the electric flash of her dark eyes. Eyes like hot chocolate syrup, he could see, now that she'd unjammed that hat from her head.

"Karen said—"

"Karen might have said it was a cabin," he pointed out, enjoying their trivial conflict. "But *I* didn't. I probably used the word 'place,' as in, 'my brother Tom's place in the Adirondack Mountains.' She must have assumed it was a cabin, as people tend to, when you mention mountains. I'm sorry if you're disappointed."

"Disappointed?" She shivered and stepped toward the warmth of the open fire, a sudden grin lighting up her face and draining away the tension in her that he still didn't understand. "Are you kidding? It's fabulous! And you even lit this fire! I've been toasting myself."

"After what you said about blazing fires and good music and hot chocolate, how could I not?"

Knowing what a panic Karen was in, he hadn't wasted time on coming into the house with Allie after he'd brought her here with baby Jane. And he'd deliberately left the fire he'd lit for her earlier to be a surprise. He didn't know, at the time, what had prompted the impulse to light it in the first place. The central heating was very efficient.

Now he understood. He'd wanted to imagine her face lighting up like that when she first saw it, and he'd gotten his reward as it lit up again now. It changed her whole personality, hinted at a warmth and softness and sense of fun that he hadn't seen much of yet in that small package of womanhood. Karen had mentioned those qualities, but he wasn't going to take them on trust. He liked to make his own decisions.

"Well, it was wonderful," she answered him. "Thank you. I haven't even tried to look around or unpack."

"You haven't made yourself that hot chocolate yet?"

"No, as I said, I've just been toasting myself. And—and Jane." She frowned.

Remembering what Karen had said about looking after her, and the rough time she'd been through— had she been ill, maybe?—he offered, "I'll make one for you, after I've taken your stuff up to your room."

"I can do that. I can make the hot chocolate, too, if you'll show me the kitchen. And I can cook dinner. Karen brought up a frozen casserole and some other stuff. While you look after Jane."

"Whatever." He shrugged.

Back to that again. She really didn't want to be with Jane, he could tell. He was aware of a disappointment nagging at his guts like stomach acid, and he took a few moments to analyze it.

Until recently he hadn't been in one place long enough to get serious about marriage to any woman, and he wasn't sure, at the moment, if he was going to be in one place for much longer. He'd been feeling a little restless lately, not totally sure that he'd made the right decision to hook up with his two brothers in their software company. There was still something missing. Something important. Maybe an intuitive voice inside him was telling him, once more, to move on.

Yet he was a family man, at heart. He had loving parents. He had seven brothers he was close to, two of whom had made happy marriages over the past couple of years. He had three little nieces of his own now. He liked extended families, loved his nieces. Deep down, he knew that his sense of family was the best medicine for the times when he had questions about himself and his life that he couldn't answer, and he didn't have any qualms about prescribing that same medicine for others.

An outwardly healthy, capable, in-control woman like this should at least *like* her own sister's child, he considered. No one was asking her to adopt the kid! What was her problem?

Fortunately, Allie hadn't noticed his look of disapproval. She was over at the window, staring out at the gathering darkness, and she didn't seem to notice his curiosity, either. How long was she going to stand there like that?

Minutes, apparently.

Jane was on her tummy on a receiving blanket spread out on the floor at a safe distance from the fire. The central heating had warmed the place up fast, as had the roaring fire in the fireplace. Jane was cooing at the leaping brightness and banging a toy. Needs fully taken care of, but utterly ignored. Allie just kept staring out the window. For some reason it seemed incredibly sad.

Instinctively, he went up to her, needing to understand her. He liked Karen a lot. She was warm, enthusiastic, full of energy and optimism...except when panicking about a jammed camera. Why was her sister so different and difficult?

He'd almost reached Allie when she turned from the window at last. "Those clouds are coming over pretty fast. Is it going to snow?"

"It's starting to look like it," he agreed. "I warned Karen about the forecast, but even half an hour ago it looked like it'd probably hold off, and she was desperate about that camera."

"She'll make it back, though, won't she? They won't close the roads. She guaranteed me she'd make it back tonight!"

The appeal and fear in her face hit him like an electric shock. "Then she'll do her best, I guess," was all he could say. It sounded lame in the face of her need.

Something about this situation had her completely terrified. Was it him? He didn't think so, but there was something. Karen's appeal to him to "look after" her suddenly made a whole lot more sense.

Karen had known Allie would feel this way. How? Why?

And why did he have such a clear, powerful intuition that the answers were going to matter to him?

Chapter Two

"Right." Allie pulled her mouth into a bright smile. "I guess you should show me my bedroom, then. It looks like there are plenty of them."

"Five," Connor said. "Six at a pinch."

"Upstairs?"

"Upstairs. You can unpack while Jane's still happy on the floor. Karen'll want the Portacrib in her room, I assume."

"I expect so."

"I'll put you in the adjoining room. Then if the storm does hit and stops Karen from getting back, you can keep the connecting door open so you'll hear Jane if she wakes in the night."

"Yes, that's the most sensible idea, isn't it?" Allie agreed, outwardly calm.

"Let's go, then."

He placed some cushions around Jane's receiving

blanket, casually betraying his experience with babies. Jane wasn't officially mobile yet, according to Karen, but she could shuffle herself backward along the floor on her tummy for quite a distance if she kept at it long enough.

"These'll keep her safely corralled while we're upstairs," Connor said.

Allie ached with envying him. Just the way he moved around the baby. Just the way he could reach down to ruffle the fuzzy, dark-gold hair on her little head without even thinking about it. Some day, with the right woman, he'd make a great dad. But for Allie, the idea of herself as a mom had become so complicated—

She snapped that compartment of her mind shut like a jailhouse gate.

Now he'd picked up the crib, the diaper bag and the soft suitcase that contained Karen's and Jane's things. Allie grabbed her overnight bag and followed him up the wide stone staircase. This was a great house, only a few years old and full of gorgeous hardwood and stone. In any other situation, she'd feel like she was on vacation here and would look forward to exploring. The house, the island, the surrounding mountains, the nearby towns.

But with Karen temporarily gone and herself and Connor and Jane trapped here by the gathering night and the prospect of a snowstorm, it felt... Well, exactly like that, as if the house were a prison, an emotional hell that wasn't her fault.

Trapped for how long? she wondered miserably. Would anything ever be truly right in her life again?

"Here you go," Connor said, opening the door of a pretty little room high in one corner of the house. It had its own bathroom and an antique Amish quilt on the bed, a connecting door to a similar room where Allie would sleep, and a little window peeping out to a white view of flat ice and snow-covered pines...and freshly falling flakes, Allie saw, already coming down thickly. Karen would be over halfway to Albany by now. Had the storm hit down that way yet?

"Any idea how to set this thing up?" Connor indicated the Portacrib in its blue nylon cover.

"No. Sorry."

She took her bag through to the connecting room, then came back and watched him helplessly as he unzipped the cover and rattled around with the legs and sides of the crib. He discovered some instructions printed on it and started muttering to himself. Since she didn't want to think too hard about having Jane so close to her during the night and what that would mean, she watched his body instead. It wasn't a punishing activity. Even without the bulk of the coat he'd been wearing outside, he looked incredibly solid and strong in his dark sweater and pants, yet he moved very easily.

Or most of him did. For the first time, she noticed that he had a slight limp and it drew her attention to the lines of his thighs and hips, defined by the dark clothing he wore. Had he hurt himself recently? Or was it something permanent, dating from long ago?

And how come it didn't detract from his masculine grace but only added to it? The limp hinted at a whole, complex range of possibilities about his past, suggesting there was a lot more to Connor Callahan than met the eye. And what met the eye was impressive enough to begin with. It was a long time since she'd met a man who wore his strength and good looks so casually, and with so little arrogance.

"Karen says you're in the computer-software business," she said, needing to know more about him. Karen had said she could trust him. That didn't mean she felt comfortable with their situation.

"Yeah." He nodded as he pushed the base of the crib into place. He had his sleeves pushed up to the elbows, and she noticed how strong his forearms were. "A couple of years ago I joined the company two of my brothers started. I head up their games division now. Tom has a pretty impressive computer up here, but I won't be powering it up this weekend."

"Karen will keep us busy as soon as she gets back." *I wish she hadn't left. That darned camera!*

"I offered her my disposable camera to take some shots with, but she wasn't impressed," Connor said. Once again, their thoughts had travelled along the same track.

"I should think not!" Allie exclaimed. "Have you any idea how she feels about that camera of hers?"

"I do now," Connor admitted humbly. "It has features I didn't know existed."

"Yes, it's some German or Swiss thing that cost her half a gazillion dollars."

"Insured, I hope."

"Definitely insured. I know she was acting a little crazy this afternoon, but my sister is actually very—"

"I know what your sister's like," he soothed, jerking the side rails of the crib upward with knotted hands to lock them straight. "A whirlwind of energy, with a heart of gold. She makes a great neighbor and a terrific mom."

"Yes, she does, doesn't she? An incredible mom." Her throat was tight again.

"She and John have become good friends since I moved in next door," Connor went on. If he'd noticed her sudden emotion, he didn't let on. "That's why I was happy to bail her out with this book-cover deal. Contrary to what my brother accused me of when I went to pick up the keys to this place, it's not 'cause I have a wild urge to be immortalized as Nancy Sherlock's answer to Rhett Butler on the front of three million copies of *Days of Grace and Danger*."

"Three million?"

"That's not unrealistic, apparently, if they go ahead with the movie," he pointed out. "Although Karen says that they might reprint the paperback using movie stills for the cover."

"Gee, you know all about it!"

"Don't you, too? She's been reading the manuscript of the book all week and giving me updates on the plot, as well as a play-by-play account of the problems with the cover design. I assumed she'd been doing the same with you."

"Karen and I... Well, we haven't spent a lot of time together lately," Allie said uncomfortably.

"Haven't you?"

He looked up. He had the crib all set up now, and had found the crib-size quilts folded in the top of Karen's suitcase. Their eyes met as he shook one out, revealing a fluffy pink-and-white-striped flannel fabric. Allie flushed, then chilled, in the space of a few seconds. She could tell quite clearly what he was thinking.

He knows it's because of Jane.

But he couldn't know *why*. Was he going to let it go?

No.

"And yet you seem close, like you really care about each other and like each other's company."

The tone was mild, but he was deliberately pushing. She could tell. And she felt angry. How *dare* he? What gave him the right to probe like that, with all the hostility and disapproval such probing implied?

She glared at him, and then—wham! It hit her like needles of hot water under a welcome shower. Like the taste of chocolate after strong, sugarless coffee. Like the rush of a summer wave on a Carolina beach. There was chemistry between them, insistent and physical, full of promise and delight. Chemistry that shattered her control, even while it made her heart dance. Chemistry that frightened her, even while it sang to her soul.

Underneath, she'd known it all along, right from the first moment she'd heard that gravelly, cream-filled and not entirely safe voice of his. Right from the moment she'd seen the startling blue eyes beneath the intimidating black hat.

And her sudden understanding of this chemistry answered the indignant question she'd just silently posed. That was what gave him the right to probe for answers from her as he was doing. Because he felt the chemistry, too.

Her breathing was shallow now, and she wanted to run a mile. She couldn't possibly dare to open up to this. She had to freeze him off. Freeze herself off, too, because there was no way she was ready to let a man into her life at this point—any man—when she had so much else to struggle with.

"We are close," she answered him frostily at last. "Which is exactly why we can take some time out from our relationship when we need to."

"And you've needed to just lately?"

"Yes." She wasn't going to explain any further. Let him think what he liked!

"Okay." He shrugged and bent to spread a second quilt on top of the first. "Cute," he commented, studying the lush, hand-quilted and machine-appliqued design of sea creatures illustrating the numbers from one to nine. He bent lower, and touched the bright beading that picked out a sea urchin's shell. "Karen made this?"

"I did." She turned deliberately away so she wouldn't see the surprise on his face as he straightened, but he didn't let it go, despite her crystal-clear signal.

"You quilt?" he sounded astonished.

The man was relentless!

"Yes," she retorted. "And I have three heads and the body of a leopard."

"Hey. Hey..." His voice had softened so that it sent hot prickles of need charging up and down her spine. "Is it a crime on my part to suggest that you seem more like a career gal?"

"Must people be purely one or the other?"

"No, of course not. But—"

"Jane's fussing," she announced abruptly, and fled from the room and down the stairs.

She only realized when she reached the bottom that it was the first time in Jane's life that she'd gone to her willingly and without an agony of turmoil, in the handful of times they'd been under the same roof. And what a tribute to Connor Callahan's effect on her equilibrium that was!

"Hi, little girl," she said softly as she entered the big, open living area and approached the glorious warmth of the fire. Janey was whimpering and fretting as if to say, "Okay, I'm done looking at the fire. Isn't somebody going to come smile at me soon, and show me something interesting? I'm bored!"

"I know," Allie answered her, as if Jane had spoken her complaint in clear English. Then, with her heart beginning to pound, she bent down and picked the baby up.

But it was too hard. "Are you looking for your...your Mommy?" she asked, her voice coming out with an unnatural intonation.

What would happen if I kissed her, just smothered

her with kisses, and smelled her little head and let her little hands grab at my clothing? Allie wondered. *What would happen?*

Unconsciously, she held Jane farther away from her and her arms were stiff and awkward. No wonder the baby writhed, arching her back and screwing up her face. She wasn't happy with such blatant ineptitude. She wanted to be held against a warm body. Who could blame her?

Allie heard Connor's footsteps behind her.

"Want me to take her?" There was a surprising amount of understanding in his voice.

"Uh, sure. I was going to get that hot chocolate, wasn't I?"

"Yup. I'll take a mug, too, while you're at it. Kitchen's back through that door."

"Two hot chocolates, coming right up. And I'll put the casserole in a low oven to start heating up while I'm at it," she planned aloud. "It must be still half-frozen, and it's already after five o'clock."

"I guess Janey, here, will want to eat early," he agreed.

He was holding her with casual, practised ease, bouncing her on his hip and earning radiant, open-mouthed smiles, entirely uncomplicated by the presence of teeth. Allie's envy and torment was like a straitjacket.

"The jars of baby food are in her diaper bag, I think," Allie said. "Is there a microwave? Because I think she likes them warmed up."

"There's a microwave. Any idea what time she eats and goes down for the night?"

"I think she's usually down by seven, but she has a bath before that, so I guess she eats at about six."

"See, kiddo," Connor crooned, "we're cookin', here. We've got your routine worked out—we know what you eat. You're not gonna miss your mommy at all, are you?"

If the gurgle was an answer, it sounded like Jane agreed.

Allie hid in the kitchen for the next half hour, apart from ten minutes spent sipping her hot drink by the fire while Connor changed a messy diaper. He made so little fuss about the task that she didn't even realize he'd done it until he dumped the diaper bag back on the end table next to the squashy cream sofa and announced, "Fresh as a daisy again."

Back in the kitchen, as she turned the oven up higher and found salad and garlic bread amongst the provisions her sister had brought, Allie wondered about Connor's new attitude. He didn't seem so hostile anymore, and there was a peacefulness in the atmosphere now. Against the night-dark sky, the snow still whirled, thick and silent, promising changed plans, but in here it was seductively cozy.

The savory aroma of the beef casserole began to snake through the house, mingling with the faint tang of wood smoke. Connor had put on some soft music, and maybe it was that or maybe it was the warmth of the fire, or just the long, travel-filled day, but Jane was getting tired.

At six, Connor came into the kitchen with the baby and announced, "No way is this little princess going to make it until seven o'clock, and I think we'd better skip any thought of a bath.''

Allie just nodded, pushing back a dangerous rush of tenderness at the sight of those rosy little cheeks and heavy lids.

"She's finished her bottle," Connor said. "I'll feed her her fruit in here, and she might be asleep before she's even done. Now, let's think. Where's the high chair?"

"There's a high chair here?"

"Believe me," he drawled, "in the Callahan family, there's always a high chair."

She laughed in sudden delight. "That's nice!"

"Is it?" He flashed her a look that was curious and ready to be convinced.

"It says something about a family, when there's always a high chair." Her face had softened with her smile.

"Yeah, *I* think so," he agreed, then added, "Actually, here there's probably two high chairs. Tom and Julie have twins, just one year old. Adorable little monsters, they are. I've been doing a fair bit of hands-on uncle-ing over the past six months or so, and I'm speaking from experience!"

"Boys?"

"Girls. My mom had eight boys. This generation, so far, is specializing in the other kind."

"Your mom must be thrilled."

"She is. And as for Dad..."

He didn't say anything further for a while, just found one of the high chairs folded away in a storage closet and brought it out. Then he sat Jane in it, put her in a bib, heated a jar of pureed apricots in the microwave, stirred and tested it carefully and began to feed her with a rubber-tipped spoon. As he'd predicted, her little head was nodding by the time he got to the bottom of the jar.

Watching him ease her gently out of the high chair, Allie asked in a distracted tone, "Shall I set the table in here, or...?"

"Nicer to eat by the fire, don't you think?"

"Uh...yes, it would be."

"Want me to take her up to bed while you start setting everything up on the hearth?"

"Thanks. Yes."

There was a tiny pause.

"Want to give her a good-night kiss?"

Another pause.

"Okay."

He brought the baby over and held her out for her kiss, his blue eyes fixed steadily and thoughtfully on Allie's face.

I've never done this before. I've never kissed her, she thought.

But she managed it, and it didn't last long, just one little press of lips—dry lips—on a soft, velvety cheek. Somehow she kept those flooding feelings dammed back.

When he'd gone, though, tiptoeing from the kitchen with Jane's head resting heavily on his shoulder and her breathing slow and even, Allie had to lean against the granite counter to keep from buckling at the knees.

Karen called while Connor was still upstairs. She

sounded tired but resigned at the far end of the phone. And Allie was resigned to what she knew the news would be.

"Where are you?" Allie demanded.

"Albany. I've just checked into a motel. Sorry I didn't call earlier, but the trip down was a nightmare. The snow started just after the Saratoga exits and, boy, did it hit thick and fast! When I got here, the camera store was about to close. I had to sweet-talk the guy into staying open and taking a look at the thing."

"How is it?"

"Fixed. He had the part. Took him half an hour. Then I started out on the Interstate to get back up to you."

"That was crazy, Karen!"

"I know. But I kept hoping maybe it hadn't gotten so heavy up there. I mean, the sky was still blue...well, half-blue...when I left! And they turned me back. They've closed the road. If the snow eases off by morning, which it's supposed to do, if I can believe the Weather Channel, they'll have plowed and I can get back."

"Plowed all the way up to—" Allie began, but Karen didn't let her finish.

"How's Jane?" she demanded.

"Asleep. Connor took her up, oh, about twenty minutes ago."

"Okay, then." Karen took a deep breath. Clearly, she wanted to ask more about the baby. Did she play? Did she take a bath? Did she seem upset? But

Karen apparently decided to hold the questions back.

She didn't say, "Kiss her for me," either, and Allie didn't tell her sister that she already had.

"I'm going to call you again first thing tomorrow," Karen promised. "And I'll give you the number here if you need to call me."

Connor came back downstairs just as Allie was winding up her conversation. He paused halfway down and for a few moments listened quite shamelessly—she'd turned and seen him, so it didn't feel like eavesdropping—intrigued by the mystery and complexity of the woman he was just beginning to get to know.

He listened to the way she handled her sister, soothing her anxieties, teasing her a little. She was clearly comfortable with their loving and supportive relationship. And yet they "hadn't spent a lot of time together lately."

He thought about the quilt she'd made for Jane, and what that said about her creativity and her care for beautiful things. I really must find out about her career, he decided. He'd been assuming it was something high-powered but rather cold. The sort of job where she'd wear a power suit, size eight, and deal with money or property or corporate clients. Accountancy or law or international banking.

But how many international bankers took the time to create a beautiful handmade quilt for their niece? And how many people, no matter what their profession, would make a quilt for a baby they couldn't even hold or touch without stiffening as if they'd been turned to ice?

He felt this overwhelming need to take her by those fine-boned shoulders and demand, "What happened to you? What damaged you? And how can I help you to heal?"

And that last question was completely insane, because he'd only known her for three hours. It didn't make any sense at all.

Abandoning the unanswerable issue, he reached the bottom of the stairs as Allie put down the phone. "Everything okay?"

"She's in Albany, at a motel. The camera's fixed," she summarized, and added a couple more details.

"Are we ready to eat? It smells great!"

"Karen's a fabulous cook."

"I know. I've tasted her chicken potpie and her lasagna."

"Her beef casserole is even better."

"Do you cook?" he couldn't help asking as they brought the food through to the hearth together. He was quite prepared to be unsurprised if she did, thinking again of the quilt, but she made a face.

"I scramble. As in eggs. I toss. As in salad. And I reheat. As in leftovers, takeout or TV dinners. That's about it."

"You live alone?"

"I have an apartment," she confirmed.

"Not the best incentive, is it, living alone?"

"Incentive?"

"For becoming a great cook."

"No," she agreed. "You need people to cook for, don't you?"

"People you care about," he said, pinpointing her meaning more exactly.

For a brief moment, their eyes met, then she looked quickly away. But not before they'd each read far too much in the other's face, by the light of soft table lamps and a glowing fire. Things you couldn't even put into words.

Then they both came to their senses and got busy dishing the gravy-rich casserole into bowls, unwrapping the garlic bread from its foil wrapping, breaking it into steaming pieces, tossing dressing onto salad, pouring a little red wine.

"Your sister hasn't mentioned what you do for a living," Connor said as they began to eat, each hunkered down on one of the squishy two-seater sofas pulled close to the hearth.

He tried to make it sound like a casual question, but for some reason he really wanted to know. He had the instinctive sense that whatever it was, he was going to be surprised.

He wasn't wrong, and when she told him, he had the answer to at least one of his many questions about this woman. He knew why, whenever he heard her voice, he felt as if they'd met before, despite the fact that he could never have forgotten meeting a woman like Allie.

"Actually, I'm a radio announcer," she said, with a grin that was almost apologetic, as if she'd already understood that he was expecting something from left field. "I do the morning drive-time program on

Philadelphia's Country Classic Radio WPYR. We Play Your Requests. We're Not the Biggest, but We're the Best." She'd dropped into her on-air voice half way through, rich and melodic and up-beat.

"Oh—my—lord!" he got out, stunned, then had to check to make sure he'd really gotten it right. "You mean you're A. J. Todd? *The* A. J. Todd?"

"Stands for Alison Jane."

"I listen to you all the time, on my way in to work. Karen never said."

"Why should she? It's a minor station, and our broadcasting range is pretty small. I'm not exactly a nationally syndicated shock jock."

No, but as far as I'm concerned, you do have the sexiest voice on American radio, bar none.

Fortunately, he hadn't said it aloud. Alone here, with the night ahead and only a six-month-old baby girl for chaperone, he didn't need to have her thinking he was coming on to her. Somehow he suspected that she could do a pretty good job of freezing a man into solid ice if she had a mind to, and though he hadn't made up his own mind what he wanted from her yet, he definitely knew it wasn't that.

He groped for something safer. "Are you ambitious, career-wise, A.J. Todd? Would you like to be a big name in radio?"

"Of course!" she answered, then paused, narrowed her eyes a little and repeated, "Of course I would," in a much less definite tone.

He sensed a little chink he could use to enter her world, the way a spelunker might slide through a crevice to find a huge, unexplored cavern system. "It's not obligatory to be ambitious, is it?" he asked.

"Well, no, but I guess I've always been the career woman in the family. Karen's doing great with her art, but family comes first for her, and always has. Clare, our younger sister, has a religious vocation and has known it since age ten."

"So you've positioned yourself as the ambitious one?"

"Positioned myself?"

"You're a middle child, right? So am I. I know the drill."

"As I understand it, there are six middle children in your family," she pointed out, a little cool.

So she didn't like this kind of analysis? Tough! Connor decided. For some reason, he really wanted her to know that she could trust him, open up to him. To the point where he was prepared to force it a little.

"Makes no difference," he answered her. "There's still the same need to fight for a unique place. In one way, that's good. In others... Well, I spent a good few years working at stuff I didn't really enjoy, just to prove a point."

"Like what?"

"You mean what point? That I was my own person, I guess."

"No, what did you work at?"

"Oh, drilling for oil in Alaska, roadying for a country-music band, doing stunt work in films.

That's how I banged up this leg, don't know if you've noticed.''

"I noticed," Allie admitted. She didn't admit that to any healthy, red-blooded female, the slight imperfection could only make him seem sexier.

She hid behind another forkful of casserole and a sip of wine. Her glass was almost empty, and she was definitely going to stop at one. She hardly ever drank alcohol, and wasn't interested in discovering how much it would take to loosen her tongue. Connor Callahan seemed to be doing a pretty good job of that, without the aid of artificial stimulants, by the cunning approach of baring his own soul!

Unfair. Totally unfair. She really didn't want to spend three hours by the fire with him, talking while they ate their meal and drank coffee, then sinking lower and lower and sleepier and sleepier into the couch. She didn't want to feel little bits of herself accidentally slipping out of her grasp as she opened up to him, like stray socks dropping from a bundle of laundry on the way from the basket to the machine.

But it happened anyway.

By the end of the evening, Connor knew that Allie had wanted a singing career at one stage, until she'd realized her voice wasn't right for that. And Allie knew that Connor still occasionally felt that he was in some kind of competition with his older brother Adam as to who was the smartest, the strongest, the best. Connor knew that Allie had learned to quilt at evening classes because she'd been too embarrassed to ask her grandmother to teach her, in case she got the inevitable, "But you're not the homemaker of the family!"

"So you weren't the only one positioning the middle sister in the Todd family as the career girl," Connor had observed on this subject.

He also knew, because he'd apparently noticed it at the time, that she'd been absent from her microphone at Radio WPYR for several months last spring and early summer. She told him she'd needed a break. Didn't tell him she'd been living in Allentown, Pennsylvania, with her parents, almost like a recluse, and for once he hadn't probed further, hadn't pushed her for details.

It was eleven o'clock when she finally announced, "I'm going to bed. Karen says Jane usually wakes up around six."

"Want me to get up with her?"

"No." She shook her head firmly. Was it the wine? She felt as if she was starting to see things a little more clearly, and with a little more confidence in herself after so many months of doubt.

Karen's news today about her pregnancy…had that changed anything? Perhaps it had changed everything.

"I'm her aunt," she said, listening to how it sounded. Did it still sound right? Had it *ever?* "Jane's my responsibility tonight, not yours."

He shrugged. "Fine by me. In that case, you get to bed, and I'll clear up."

"You sure?"

"I'm your host. It's my responsibility, not yours," he said, mimicking her tone and choice of words. She was grateful to him for putting a little distance between them once more.

A few moments later, she'd begun to head up the stairs, knowing exactly why she was reluctant to go, and getting more scared by the minute about just how she'd handle tomorrow if the snow kept on falling.

"If Karen has a hidden agenda for this weekend," she muttered aloud, "She couldn't have planned this situation better if she'd tried!"

Chapter Three

The sounds of cooing and gurgling drew Allie out of a deep sleep, and it took her a minute or two to make sense of them, and of where she was.

Then, as she swam up to the surface of wakefulness, she remembered.

This was Connor's brother's place in the Adirondack Mountains. And that was Jane, in the very next room, awake and talking. She'd awoken once in the night, also, but had settled herself back to sleep after a few minutes of fretting. Now she sounded content, alone in her crib, but that wouldn't last forever.

Allie folded back the bedding and set her bare feet down on the hard, chilly wooden floor. Padding over to the window, she looked out into darkness but couldn't tell if the snow was still falling. She took a shower in the adjoining bathroom and dressed in close-fitting blue sweatpants and a matching baggy top, thick cherry-colored socks and a pair of white leather trainers.

Jane was getting noisier. It was that same *I'm bored* fretfulness that Allie had learned to recognize yesterday afternoon.

"Shh!" Allie told her softly. "Let's not wake Connor, hey?"

She bent over the crib and picked the baby up, and felt little hands immediately clutch the fabric of her sweatshirt.

Oh, she was so warm! She wore a little pastel-toned flannel nightdress that Karen had sewed herself, with a drawstring at the bottom that could be pulled tight to make a kind of sleeping bag, keeping little bootee-clad feet extra toasty. The urge and instinct to cuddle her, welling deep inside Allie, was so strong that she gave into it fully and held the little bundle tight, feeling the silken hair against her cheek. Oh, silk, satin, what other words could you use to describe such a darling, precious bundle as this!

Oh, help, help!

It was a quarter past six in the morning. Allie had no strength at this hour, no willpower. How could she do anything but give in to this overpowering need?

"Let's go down and get that diaper changed," she told the baby in a shaky voice. She didn't wait for an answering coo, just tiptoed quickly down the stairs and into the kitchen, where she figured the light and the noise wouldn't disturb Connor.

And I should give her a bath, she decided.

She felt clumsy and totally lacking in experience. If Jane was going to have a bath, then she needed a towel. And of course she needed clean clothing, too, which Allie had left upstairs as well. She started back up with a bare baby bottom parked on her arm, as she didn't dare to leave Jane downstairs and diaperless on her own.

Towel, clothing, ointment…was there anything else? Yes, a spare sterilized bottle. Those were still upstairs. Where was the formula? In the kitchen? Jane must be hungry, though she hadn't yet begun to complain.

I don't know what I'm doing!

And she'd probably waken Connor at any moment. In this direction, on her way to her room, she could glimpse him through the slightly open doorway of his room, a dark hump in the bed, breathing deeply and rhythmically.

Help me!

Was she praying, or simply willing him to wake up? He didn't, and she got safely back downstairs with everything she needed.

There was a deep sink in the laundry room that would serve as a bathtub. Holding the baby, she ran the faucet, testing it for temperature. Too hot? Too cool? What was that thing capable mothers did with droplets on the inside of their wrist? Or was that only for testing the temperature of bottles?

And in all of this, the practical ineptitude and clumsiness she felt was the easy part. Oh, very definitely the easy part! It was the emotion coursing through her that was hard.

Love.

Oh lord, she *loved* this baby! *Her* baby, not Karen's. Hers, born from her body, made from her, nourished by her, although she'd told herself months ago that she had to learn never to think of that, she had to learn to let Jane belong to Karen, and to believe that everything had worked out for the best.

Did she still feel that way? Yesterday, Karen had given her permission to ask this huge question, but how did she even start to answer it?

When Jane was clean and fresh and dressed, Allie sat at the kitchen table and gave her a bottle. She was hardly aware of the enthusiastic sucking sounds and the trilling of the bubbles as they formed in the rapidly disappearing creamy liquid. Instead, her mind plunged back into the memory of her labor, six months earlier.

Twenty-eight hours of pain and slow progress, before her doctor had finally assisted Jane's entry into the world with vacuum extraction.

She was a big baby. Well over nine pounds, which Allie's small frame just wasn't meant for. And yet, miracle of miracles, after all her anger and uncertainty, her consideration of adoption and even a termination of the pregnancy, Allie had felt such an overwhelming rush of euphoric tenderness, just for a few short minutes.

"A girl? You mean it's a girl? When I had the ultrasound, you thought—"

The obstetrician looked at her over his glasses, his pale face stern. She'd never particularly liked him on her prenatal visits, but hadn't thought to change to someone else, since not liking her obstetrician seemed like the least of her worries.

"The ultrasound suggested a boy," he said. "At twenty weeks' gestation, it's not always possible to be definite. In this case, I was wrong. Does it make a difference to you? Did you want a girl?"

But Allie hadn't gotten the chance to reply, either to Dr. Leith or for herself. She'd started losing blood, a dramatic postpartum hemorrhage that had ended in an emergency blood transfusion and two days of weakness and utter exhaustion. That wasn't the end of it. An infection had set in, resistant to antibiotics, and for a while her life had been on the line. It was almost three weeks before she was able to leave the hospital, and by that time Jane had been discharged into Karen's care...and into Karen's heart.

This had been the plan she and Karen had talked about during the final weeks of the pregnancy. And so the tiny-yet-insistent voice inside her which had said, during those first few precious moments after Jane's birth, "You can change your mind. She's yours. You can keep her," went unheeded.

Allie didn't dare to look at the possibility that if she hadn't had the postpartum hemorrhage and infection, she might have kept Jane, might have loved her. The near-fatal bleeding episode had seemed like a sign that she'd made the right decision.

And when she remembered the anger and ambivalence she'd felt so many times about the life inside her through the pregnancy and labor, she could only shudder with dread. She hadn't been ready for a baby in her life yet, even one conceived in the best of circumstances.

But Jane had not been conceived that way. She'd been conceived in the middle of a nightmare.

"I've done the right thing," Allie had told herself a thousand times since. "Because if I ever found myself feeling toward Jane a particle of the anger and loathing that I feel toward her father..."

And from the moment she had first held her, Karen had loved Jane like her own child, unburdened by any personal reason for anger toward an innocent being.

She and John had been trying for over four years to conceive. They'd been told there was no obvious medical reason why it hadn't happened, and that they should just keep trying and be patient. But Karen had found such patience very hard, and ultimately, in the face of her sister's infertility, Allie hadn't been able to contemplate a termination.

But now Karen was successfully pregnant at last, and she'd said all along that if Allie ever changed her mind...

Was it fair? Was it safe? Was it too late?

Oh, this was so hard!

Wiping tears from her face with the heel of her hand, Allie looked down into the baby's face. Jane had finished her bottle and had formula creaming on her lips as she gurgled and cooed once more.

"What's it like, Jane?" Allie whispered. "What's it like to be in a world that's so new? Everything for you is new, isn't it? As far as you're concerned, the calendar started at Day One when you were born. There's no past, no baggage, and when I look at you, smiling like that—oh, your smile!—I can get a glimpse of it, too. A life with no baggage. Starting all over again. With you.''

A second later, Jane had stopped smiling and begun to writhe. Allie didn't understand, until she remembered about tummy gas. She lifted the little girl up to her shoulder and thumped her back gently until the trapped air escaped and Jane was happy again.

Footsteps sounded on the stairs. *Oh, damn! Connor.*

And my eyes are still a mess.

She fled through the door into the laundry room just as he entered the kitchen, and hoped she'd made it in time. Had he seen her smeared tears and reddened lids? She couldn't bear to have him guess at the dark, conflicting feelings that were twisted like braided rope inside her.

''Hi,'' she said, as casually as a squeezed throat would permit. ''Just changing a diaper here.''

''Congratulations.''

''I beg your pardon?''

''Didn't you tell me yesterday that you'd never done it before? Now you're up to about number three, aren't you? I count that as an achievement on your part.''

''I guess I have a steep learning curve,'' she joked. ''I could do it in my sleep now.''

''Then I'll look forward to watching your progress in other areas. You'll have written a manual on child care by the time Karen gets back.''

"Don't count on it." The humor was forced, and Allie heard the strain in her own voice.

I didn't used to be this person. So tight and scared and doubting, hurting so bad without an answer. Will I get it right in the end?

Her fingers on the tapes of the disposable diaper were so clumsy that she had to fasten them three times before she got them to stick in the right spot. The only good thing about taking so long at the task was that by the time she'd finished, she knew her eyes weren't red anymore.

What Allie didn't know was that Connor had seen her face in telltale profile several minutes earlier, as she went through into the laundry room. And he'd seen how red-rimmed were those deep, liquid chocolate pools that intrigued him so. Crying.

He didn't know why. In a way, it didn't even matter. What mattered far more was the effect her tears had on him. He'd never felt such a huge need to step in and do whatever it took to make a woman forget her sadness and her fear. While she fiddled with the diaper—oh yes, he'd heard those tapes being ripped open and stuck down again, to the accompaniment of muttered curses—he'd plotted all the possible ways he could cheer her, distract her.

For a start, breakfast. It was obvious she hadn't yet eaten. There were no dishes in the sink. It was only seven-thirty and the sun was just up, shedding light on a blue and white and gold world. The storm had spent itself and moved on.

Tom and Julie kept this place pretty well stocked

for winter visits. There were eggs and bacon in the refrigerator and waffles and breakfast sausages and hash browns in the freezer. Allie was so fine-boned. If she had been sick—and sometimes there was a look to her which told him she had been; she was pale when her cheeks weren't painted pink with cold—then she needed building up. One hearty breakfast on its way!

Two, actually. He wasn't a man who expected his guests to eat alone.

The phone rang.

"I'll get it. It'll be Karen," Allie said quickly.

"I'll take the baby," he offered.

"Thanks."

But the word didn't have quite the same heartfelt relief in it, poorly disguised, that it would have had yesterday. Connor tucked this observation away in his mind, not quite sure what to do with it. He had the feeling, though, that he'd need it later on.

Allie handed Jane to Connor and hurried out to the phone in the living area. When she heard Karen's voice, she could tell right away that something was wrong.

"Are you still at the motel?"

"No, I'm about thirty miles away, at the police station in Wayans Falls." Shaky and tearful.

"Karen, what happened?"

"I woke up early and could see that the snow had stopped. I could hear the snow plows going up and down the city streets. I figured they'd have plowed the Interstate, and the county roads, too, by the time I reached them. But the county roads weren't plowed, so I parked on the shoulder of it before I got stuck. Then the plow came along and... I guess I'd parked in a really dumb spot...the minivan got totaled.''

''What?''

''By the snowplow,'' Karen clarified.

Unnecessarily.

Allie had a horrible vision of the event, complete with the sound of crunching metal. She could only thank heaven that Karen had not, apparently, been inside the vehicle at the time.

''So they brought me back here,'' Karen finished. ''And gave me some medicinal brandy.'' She gave a slightly hysterical hiccup. ''Even if I go to the car-rental place at Wayans Falls airport, the snowplow guys told me they won't get to 357 till, probably, tomorrow morning. And if you could just shoot me now, Allie, before Nancy Sherlock and that huge multinational publisher of hers do it for you, I'd be deeply grateful! The good news is, the camera's okay.''

She ended on a laugh that was half a sob, and Allie did the heroic thing, took a deep breath and assumed the role of strong sister.

It felt strange, so strange.

She'd often been the strong sister in the past. ''The pint-size dynamo,'' Dad used to call her sometimes. She was the one who'd ordered Karen to show her future husband, John, how she felt about him at a point where it looked like their relationship was going nowhere. She was the one who'd told various men what lake they could go jump in when they'd tried coming on to her sister Clare—men who regarded Clare's planned commitment to an order of Carmelite nuns as a personal challenge to their manhood.

But for the past year or so, since discovering her pregnancy, she hadn't been strong. Not really. And she was rusty at it.

"Okay, here's what we're going to do," she told Karen.

When she put down the phone a few minutes later, she felt a new and satisfying sense of inner strength starting to return. And she found that Connor was leaning in the doorway that led through to the kitchen, watching her with that intent, thoughtful expression she'd already come to know. He had Jane on his hip and a pancake flipper in his hand.

"I heard," he said.

"Do you mind that I requisitioned your camera?"

"I offered it yesterday, if you remember."

"She's a lot more desperate today. She accepted."

"We'll take as many different types of shots as we can, after breakfast," he said. "Hopefully there'll be something she can use, even if she doesn't get the chance to take anymore."

"Breakfast?"

"It's ready. The full meal deal. Looks darned cold out there, so we're going to need it."

"Brrr!" Allie shivered in anticipation, and wrapped her arms around herself.

"Not looking forward to it?"

"Not wildly."

"Hey," he teased softly. "Chin up, A.J. Todd. It's going to be fun!"

And as she felt his blue-eyed gaze sweeping over her, still lit by that glint of easy humor, she had a sudden rush of crazy, unaccountable confidence that he'd turn out to be right.

Chapter Four

"Okay, now, say cheese," Connor ordered.

He had the disposable camera ready, with Allie and Jane posed against a snow-covered pine in some of the pioneer-style costumes Karen had brought with her.

"I don't think Karen wants cheese," Allie answered. "Isn't Nancy Sherlock's writing generally pretty intense?"

"You're right," Connor said. "Okay, say sauerkraut instead—hell, we don't know what we're doing here, do we?"

"Not a clue," she agreed simply.

She hugged Jane closer. They were both well-wrapped, in swaddling blankets and a couple of thick woollen shawls, but the diamond-clear day was so cold it seemed the air itself might shatter. Beneath Connor's boots, the snow squeaked as he paced back and forth, thinking.

"Do you know what?" he finally said.

"What?"

"We're going to forget that this is supposed to be for the cover of a book that neither of us have read. We're not going to try and take on characters or create a mood. We've only got one roll of film. We're just going to take pictures, as if this was *us*, on vacation in the mountains and having a ball."

And so they did. Connor clicked off three shots of Allie and the baby before she even realized he was doing it, so he got her frowning down at Jane and pulling her blankets more closely around her face, then staring accusingly at the camera, her bundled shawls and frozen hair making her look like a wild woman.

He had her standing on her own, a dark, solitary figure in her long, old-fashioned skirts, against the bright blue and white of the lake and the sky. He told her, "Take Jane for a ride on the sled," and took shots of her pulling Jane along the ice, strapped sitting up on the old Flexible Flyer he'd unearthed from the shed.

Next, Allie had her revenge. She made him climb on top of a big stack of firewood, then split some kindling while she photographed him in action, the ax swinging rhythmically above his head and then down again.

"Killing two birds with one stone," she said. "I noticed the box of kindling by the fireplace was almost empty."

Jane thought Connor's chopping was hilarious, so Connor dropped the ax in the snow and grabbed the camera. He took her bouncing in Allie's arms and still laughing in delight, her mouth wide open, her eyes bright and Allie's face both beaming and tender as she shared the innocent baby happiness.

Finally, on an impulse, he pulled the two of them close into the shelter of one arm and held the camera out at arm's length in his other hand, pointed it in what he hoped was the right direction and began to click.

First, he caught her startled expression, then the spark of awareness that ignited in her eye, and lastly—heaven only knew what made him give in to this impulse—he captured her shocked recognition of the imminent reality of his kiss as he bent his head to brush her mouth with his.

Connor's kiss lasted only a moment, but its effect was shattering. Allie felt her whole body tighten. Her breathing, her stomach muscles, even her scalp. Moments later, the tightening effect was reversed in a shower of tingles that ran the length of her body as she began to melt inside.

His nose had felt cold against her cheek, but his lips were so warm, protected by the upturned collar of his Civil-War-style greatcoat, which had scratched and tickled against her cheek. She felt her eyes widen as he stared down at her, his face still just an inch or two from hers. The tip of his tongue rested thoughtfully between his front teeth and his bottom lip, and he'd forgotten all about the camera.

Allie hadn't.

"I think that's enough, don't you?" she said

breathlessly, her whole body rigid and screaming rebellion, although she fought mightily to keep it from showing. "Must have just about shot off the whole roll."

"Two shots left," he growled, the syrup in his voice drizzling thickly over the roughness underneath. "I haven't read it, but Karen's told me the plot. Definitely a romance. I think we need to do that again."

"Why? You weren't clicking while we did it last time." His arm was still around her, holding her close. She swallowed her panic, battled her need to twist out of his arms.

"Which is why we need to do it again," he pointed out softly. Between them, Jane was cooing and singing, looking happily back and forth from one to the other as if to say, "Thanks for the entertainment, guys, and you're keeping me nice and warm, too."

Connor's mouth had broken into a slow, seductive grin. He was enjoying this moment, apparently, and wasn't afraid to let Allie know it. Why should he be, when her first, instinctive response had been so obviously positive?

"Only two shots," he said. "Won't take long. Just give us a second to get into position."

His mouth moved closer again as he spoke, so that there was a mere whisper of space between her lips and his. She could feel herself nearly drowning in his eyes. Panic warred with need inside her. She could have scraped her chin on his overnight growth of stubble. She could have given short shrift to any nonsense about closed mouths by parting her lips, reaching up a hand to pull on his jaw and pressing herself seductively against him.

"No!" she said instead and twisted away from him, giving in to the panic, her breathing jerky and uneven, pluming white in the icy air. "We don't need to. We've got enough. Jane's going to be ready for her nap soon. I have to get her out of this nineteenth-century stuff and back into her own clothes, and she'll want a bottle."

She began to walk toward the house as she spoke, trying to give a clear signal that she wasn't open to changing her mind. The heavy skirts of her costume dragged in the drifted snow, acquiring a pretty lace pattern of powdery crystals.

Jane began to whimper and grumble, lending the weight of truth to Allie's hasty excuses. She did need her bottle and her nap.

After Allie had gone about ten paces she instinctively looked back, to find Connor still standing there at the lake edge, the camera dangling forgotten in his hand. He was staring after her with narrowed eyes, and it took all her determination to turn back again and keep going, instead of giving in to the shaky mess of feelings inside her and...and...blurting out some sort of...Lord, what? Apology? Explanation?

There wasn't one, because she didn't have the slightest idea what was going on inside her. All she knew was that it felt terrifying, as sudden and unwelcome as last night's storm. Unlike the storm, however, it lacked any prospect of bringing the morning-after beauty of color and light that now surrounded her.

Deliberately, Allie absorbed herself totally in caring for Jane over the next half hour. After changing back into her own regular clothes, she took refuge in the baby's room. The only clue as to what Connor was doing came from the powerful, rhythmic thwack of an ax on wood down by the pile of logs. It was strangely resonant and musical in the cold, clear air. Allie didn't dare to contemplate what feelings he might be working off with all that physical labor.

Didn't dare to consider that she might be working off a few feelings, either, as she focused on the baby. She changed Jane's clothing and her diaper, keeping her from crying with fatigue by making silly faces. The surge of love and tenderness she felt every time Jane laughed or reached for her with those little hands already seemed far less frightening than it had yesterday.

Her heart was overflowing with warm, sweet liquid. She felt teary and trembly and happy...and at the same time horribly churned up over Connor.

Try not to think about that! Don't think of that kiss!

Allie fed Jane and then put her in the Portacrib with a toy and pulled the soft quilt over her.

Outside, the sound of chopping had stopped. When Allie let herself quietly out of Jane's room and stood for a moment on the landing at the top of the stairs, she could hear Connor in the kitchen. Boots creaking to and fro, faucet opening and closing, fridge door wheezing shut.

I don't want to see him.

There wasn't even Jane as a miniature chaperone to deflect the tension between them now.

All at once, the pent-up tension inside her gave way and she rebelled against the powerlessness of her situation. There had to be a way out of this. If Karen couldn't get back, then at least could Allie and Connor and Jane get out? Even if it had to be on foot?

There was no longer any point to their being here. They had a lot of gear. As long as they could bring the essentials for the baby, it didn't matter if the rest of their things, and Karen's, had to be left here for another day.

Allie began to calculate and plan.

This morning, over Connor's feed-an-army breakfast, she had asked him about those houses at the far end of the lake. Yes, some of them were occupied all year round, he'd said. They were only a mile from Route 11N at that end of the lake, and it got plowed pretty promptly because it was a county bus route.

It hadn't clicked when he said it, because Jane had conked herself in the head with a hard plastic rattle at that moment and they'd both been distracted with soothing away her tears.

But now she thought, *Why on earth, if we're just a half mile of frozen lake from a village that's only one mile from a plowed bus route, don't we get out that way?*

They could get as far as Wayans Falls and at least reunite Karen with her...daughter?

No, she's my daughter! Is it too late to have her back?

Immediately, the agony she felt over this looming decision was a distraction and a further strain on her emotions.

All these questions hitting me at once. I don't need to be alone with a man who sets my senses on fire when I don't want him to. There's no room in my life for that. That panic I felt with him just now tells me everything I need to know. I still can't trust myself as a mother, yet I can't fully trust that Karen and I made the right decision. How can I possibly trust any man as a lover...or even as a friend...after what happened fifteen months ago?

She hardly noticed that she'd grabbed her coat and hat and put them on as these thoughts came. She tiptoed down the stairs. Connor was still in the kitchen. Fixing coffee, maybe? She didn't wait to find out.

Outside, the houses at the far end of the lake beckoned, and she modified her hazy, panicky plan again.

She set off alone across the lake, half-blinded by the sun. It was almost noon, and the snow reflected the light with painful brilliance. She pulled her hat down over her eyes. That helped. But it meant that she could see only a few yards ahead, and Allie had no warning of imminent disaster. Her hearing was the first of her senses to alert her, and by then it was already too late.

Beneath her feet, the ice suddenly groaned ominously, the sound spreading rapidly away from her in all directions. A second later, there was a pool of slush-gray water opening around her, and before she could do more than turn back in a panic toward the island, she was through the ice and in the water.

She had room for just one desperate, terrified, remorseful thought. *I can't die! I can't leave Jane without a mother! And I'm her mother! I want to be her mother. I've lost six months of her precious life already....*

But Connor had seen her.

He'd heard her stealing down the stairs and had emerged from the kitchen just in time to see her let herself out of the house. He'd gone to a window and searched for her in vain amongst the snow-covered pines. Then finally he saw her dark, tiny figure at last, out on the ice and heading toward the houses on the far side.

On the ice!

Anyone who regularly came to Diamond Lake in winter knew that the ice wasn't safe in that direction. This island was close to the lake's northern shore. The water between it and the shore in that direction was shallow and motionless enough to freeze rapidly to a safe thickness.

To the south, though, it was a very different story. The lake bottom shelved steeply downward, and the fast-flowing stream that fed it from the eastern side created a slow yet persistent current that in summer would transport a child's inflatable toy reliably toward the southern shore. In winter, the deep, moving water there resisted freezing for far longer. It made a silent and deadly barrier at least fifty yards wide, across the whole lake, between the island and the southern shore.

After the thaw during the past week, it would take at least another day of this bone-snapping cold to make it safe, even for someone as light as Allie.

And she didn't know.

He clattered back down the stairs, his mind moving even faster than his feet, his old leg injury already nagging at him. It wouldn't slow him down, but it was going to hurt after this.

"I'm coming for you, Allie!"

She heard his voice, an urgent bellow across the ice, blessedly near.

He must have seen her before she fell, because there was no way he could have gotten this close in such a short time otherwise. Only a half minute…maybe less…had passed since she'd fallen through.

He was prepared, too.

Pitting her will against the frigid water that seemed to want deliberately to drag her down, Allie hardly had time to take in what was happening. Connor was stretched out flat on the ice, and something was coming spinning toward her, followed by a snaking line of rope. One end was held in his hand, the other was tied to this thing hurtling her way.

It was the sled they'd used this morning, she realized as it reached her.

"Grab it," he shouted. "Stretch out your arms. Get yourself flat. Don't try to climb onto it or you'll just keep breaking the edge of the ice. I don't dare get any closer..."

"Okay," she croaked.

Even her voice seemed to have turned to ice, and her jaw was wired shut by cold. She could hardly get out that one word, but she understood what he wanted. She needed to spread her weight. She need to try keeping as close to the surface of the water as she could so that eventually, as Connor used the attached rope to pull her toward him, where the ice was a little thicker, she would stop breaking its edge as she went and could slide onto it to safety.

For the first few yards he pulled slowly and the ice kept breaking, seeming to taunt her with its refusal to hold her, then at last it thickened enough to hold and she was sliding on her stomach like a human broom brushing the snow aside. Connor could pull her much faster now.

It didn't take long, but by the time she reached him he had to pull her to her feet. He left the sled where it lay and bundled a huge, down-filled comforter around her.

"I know you're still wet. No time to take off your stuff. At least this way you won't lose any more body heat."

He spoke as he lifted her into his arms and she didn't protest. She knew her own legs could not have carried her to the house. His progress through the deep snow at the lake edge and on the island itself was steady and slightly lopsided, and after a minute of it she heard his throat rasping each time his weight landed on his left leg. Dimly, she realized that this was hurting his old injury, but there wasn't a thing she could do about it.

The sensation of cold was ebbing now, not because she was any warmer but because her body was shutting down, ceasing to register sensation. She understood in a hazy way what Connor had realized more urgently—if she wasn't properly and carefully warmed soon, her fall through the ice could still be fatal.

The process was slow and painful. He had to undress her like a stiff-limbed baby, in front of—but not too close—to the fire, because too much heat too quickly was dangerous, also. She was too drained and fogged to fully appreciate the care he took. And she didn't care about the moments when he was forced to touch and see her bare, wet skin. What did that intimacy matter when he was in the process of saving her life? And yet she understood, even then, how her memories of his touch would haunt her later on.

Leaving her wrapped in the damp comforter and warning her about the danger of trying to warm herself too rapidly with the radiant heat of the flames, he found her spare clothes, including a huge sweater of his own, and a second downy comforter, bone-dry.

Feeling was coming back into her hands and feet now, and they ached and stung agonizingly as the nerve endings revived. When he made her some hot, sweet chocolate, she couldn't hold the mug and he had to feed it to her, tipping the china rim against her lips and watching her carefully as she sipped, so that he didn't make her splutter.

The ice that had encrusted his chest and arms from her wet clothing had melted from his black sweatshirt and was dripping down onto his jeans, but he didn't seem to notice that.

It was twenty minutes before she could speak, and even then the words came out through numb lips. "I'm s-sorry. I'm so sorry!"

"Hell, no! I should have told you the ice wasn't safe," he growled. "It was my fault, Allie." He swore. Mild words, passionate tone. "If I hadn't seen you before you fell..."

"You were—"

"Right behind you, waiting for it to happen, going as far and fast as I dared, yelling, but you had that thick hat pulled down and you didn't hear." He massaged his left thigh as he spoke, and winced a little at the pain.

"I'm sorry. Your leg."

"Don't worry about it. Won't hurt for long." He picked up his narrative once more. "You were going at a cracking pace. You looked like you were trying to escape from the hounds of hell. When you fell, I'd just gotten to the point where I didn't dare go farther. Didn't you see that the ice was getting thinner? It starts to look grayish beneath the snow. I could even see cracks."

"The sun was in my face. I wasn't thinking about it. On the other side of the island, it's thick enough for the snowmobile."

"I should have told you," he repeated.

"Is your leg going to be okay?"

"It's fine. Hurts a little. It'll stop soon. But what the hell were you doing out there?"

"Trying to find out if the road to those houses had been plowed, and if the bus you told me about was running along 11N. I thought—"

"Didn't you think I'd have suggested it, if it had been a possibility?" he asked quietly, showing more restraint than he needed to. She deserved some anger from him. "To get to that side of the lake in winter by foot, you have to go right around the edge. It's wilderness—a good four miles of thick forest and rocks."

"Connor, I'm so sorry. I guess I wasn't thinking," she admitted. "I thought I was. I thought I was planning brilliantly, but—"

"It doesn't matter. I guess I know why...one of the reasons...why you weren't at your brilliant best just now."

His sapphire-blue eyes looked deliberately into hers and his dark eyebrows were raised as if he were asking a silent question. He spoke slowly. "I have to apologize for taking advantage—"

"You didn't," she retorted, lifting her chin. "It was mutual. But that doesn't mean it's going to happen again. My life at the moment—"

"Like mine," he agreed. Now his brows had lowered into a scowl. "I'm not sure, you see..."

"I'm sorry?"

"Too much." He shook his head, then said, to make it clearer, "There's too much I'm not sure of, about where I'm headed."

"That doesn't stop a lot of men," she pointed out.

"Well, I'm happy for them," he drawled cynically. "But it stops me. If I'm not going to be in Philly much longer, I don't want to start something I can't finish."

She nodded slowly, absorbing this attitude. They were only a few throwaway words, but they revealed a lot about the man who sat so close to her, keeping her wrapped in a comforter and warming her with the pressure of his hands.

Fire, feathers, hot chocolate, hands. She was being hit by an onslaught of gentle warmth on all fronts, yet she still felt cold.

"Some chicken soup?" he suggested, and she nodded gratefully.

It didn't take him long to open a can and heat two mugs of soup in the microwave, one for each of them. Holding the mug herself this time, Allie began to feel human again, alive, safe...until she heard Jane awaken and begin to cry upstairs. Then it suddenly hit her, the same way it had hit her in the lake—she'd risked her life, and she couldn't do that. Not ever, never again, now that there was Jane.

"Connor, if you hadn't seen me, if you hadn't gotten to me in time... How could I have done that?"

She flung the comforter aside, set the soup mug down on the hearth so roughly that some of its contents slopped over the sides. Her voice was a rasping whisper through her drum-tight throat.

"I'll bring her down. How could I have left her?

How could I have risked myself like that, when there was Jane? Oh, Connor!''

Tears burned in her eyes, blinding her, and she didn't see Connor's movement, just felt his grip closing on her arm, warm, deliberate and demanding.

"Wait!'' he said. "What is it with you and Jane? You've got to tell me the truth now, Allie. I deserve that, don't I? After what we've been through?''

"I guess you do,'' she answered.

"Jane's yours, isn't she? I started to wonder this morning.... That's the only reason you could be feeling this way. The only reason you'd phrase it like that. Yet you don't have Jane with you. You've given her to your sister to raise. Maybe that's what you were running from in the first place, the enormity of that, not from me and that kiss we shared at all. The fact that Jane is yours.''

"Yes, she's mine,'' Allie said. "Jane is mine.'' It was the first time she'd ever said those words aloud. "She's my baby,'' she repeated starkly. "And I still don't know what I'm going to do about it.''

Chapter Five

"Tell me about it, Allie," Connor said.

The words were slow, soft, almost lazy, but they weren't a suggestion, they were a command, and she had to admit that he deserved it. He'd said so himself.

Saving someone's life gave a person certain rights over that someone. Namely, the right to understand how she'd gotten herself into such a senseless, dangerous situation in the first place. Of course he'd have suggested getting out via the southern end of the lake, if it had been possible! Now that she was thinking a little more sensibly, it seemed obvious.

And Allie could see now that Jane was at the heart of it, at least as much as Connor's kiss, more than her concern for Karen's book-cover deal.

Allie had brought Jane downstairs and she'd stopped crying. She was sitting there on the rug, fresh and fully awake, playing with her toys and babbling. In Allie's eyes, she was the most beautiful baby who ever lived, and getting more so every minute.

"Tell you about it," she echoed to Connor, dragging her eyes from her baby. "Just like that?"

"Isn't that the best way?" he suggested. "It'll only make it worse if we drag it out, I guess."

"What makes you think you have the right—" she blustered, as if she hadn't just conceded inwardly that he did have every right to demand that she open up to him.

Still, when he disclaimed that right, and offered her other reasons for why she should talk to him, she was surprised.

"I'm here, is all," he said. "And I'm the only person here, and you're ready, I think. Something's happened to you. Your world has just shattered into a thousand pieces, and the pattern they've landed in is different to how your life was when you woke up this morning. Don't you have to talk about it?"

He was right. Oh damn, *damn,* he was right. The truth about her past and a decision about her future were both boiling inside her, ready to spill, and somehow she didn't even mind that Connor was the person who would hear it all.

So she told him about Jerry Purcell, one of the technical team at her radio station when she started there two years ago. She would never have called him a friend, didn't know what to call him now, refused to call him the father of her child, although he undoubtedly was.

But she'd at least thought, until fifteen months ago, that he was a pleasant enough guy. He could be fun sometimes, moody at others. He always remembered people's birthdays. He joined in the camaraderie of the radio station and yet, still, somehow, he wasn't one of life's big winners.

Although he'd never before come on to her in any way—he was married, for one thing—she wasn't totally surprised that night at the end of October when he'd showed up at her place. She'd had an instinctive sense that he could be needy.

Just a shoulder to cry on? She'd thought so at first, and she'd listened to him with sympathy. It turned out that not only was he on the brink of a divorce, which had to be hard, but he'd just lost his job at the station. Even today, she didn't know why that was. He hadn't said at the time, and she hadn't asked her co-workers later, because by then she couldn't bear even to say his name.

She could still remember with perfect clarity how he'd put his arms around her after their talk, how he'd tried to kiss her. She'd edged out of his embrace, said something careful about the late hour and how she hoped their talk had helped and that he'd be okay getting home.

He'd been drinking a little before he arrived, she could tell, but that was nearly two hours earlier and now he must have sobered up.

Not sober enough, according to him. He needed a coffee. So she made one for him and one for herself, to take the edge off a heart-to-heart that had started to make her uneasy. After they'd finished the hot drink, he came at her again with his hands and his mouth, and this time her rebuff had to be firmer. He just wasn't getting the message.

She could still recall his exact words. "Don't worry, you'll relax in a minute, and we're going to have a beautiful time together." But that was her last clear memory of that night.

When she awoke the next morning, mind clear but head pounding, he had gone, but she knew what must have happened after he drugged her coffee. A woman couldn't be in any doubt. The unmistakable signs of his violation, although it hadn't been rough, left her nauseated, and her awareness of the timing of it filled her with dread.

The days went by and her fears were confirmed. She did a pregnancy test, and it was positive. At the station, no one had seen Jerry or knew where he had gone to. Someone said he had left town. She told Karen the bare bones of the story—less, even, than she was telling Connor now—and Karen suggested she try to track him down, confront him with her pregnancy.

But that was the last thing Allie had wanted.

The worst moment, perhaps, was when her obstetrician had predicted a boy, following the sonogram at twenty weeks. It was hard to imagine a boy without seeing Jerry's face, the distinctive pattern of his facial hair, the male prominence of his Adam's apple.

It was ironic, really. She'd always had a special place in her heart for active, mischievous little boys. Tentatively picturing herself as a mom someday, many years down the track, once she'd gone as far as she could with her career, she had always seen herself with a game-for-anything, gap-toothed little man-child. Dark hair, blue eyes, looking just like his daddy.

Where had that picture gone to?

When she gave birth to Jane, she still hadn't reached a final resolution on the issue of her child's future. Earlier, more than once, Karen had offered to bring up the baby—"You know how much I'm longing to be a mom. I'd love the baby with all my heart, Allie, even if you find that you can't. Wouldn't it be the best way for all of us?"

Then Allie's extended postpartum illness had settled the question with a dramatic finality that left her weak and exhausted for months. Karen had taken the baby and chosen her name. Allie still hadn't fully recovered her strength, still took iron tablets daily and got tired if she didn't get enough rest.

"But now," she finished to Connor, speaking in a cracked whisper, "Karen is pregnant at last. It's as if that fact has opened a door that I'd told myself was locked for good, with the key lost or thrown away. And I've spent this past twenty-four hours or more with Jane. I've let myself love her, as I've loved her all along without ever admitting it to myself. And everything inside me is saying, 'You can take her back. She's yours. You can have her.' Only that isn't true...is it?"

She looked up at him at last, her voice pleading, though why she expected him to have an answer for her, she didn't know.

And he didn't have an answer, only another question. Blunt. Demanding.

"Why isn't it true?"

"Why? Surely it's obvious!"

"Tell me! Put it into words, Allie."

"Because if I let myself think about her father, for even a single moment... I was so angry. There were so many times during the pregnancy when I was angry."

"But have you ever felt one moment of that anger toward *her,* since she was born? Have you, Allie?"

She thought about it, although she didn't really need to, then finally answered him slowly, "No. No, I haven't. Of course I haven't."

"And you won't," he suggested softly, almost hypnotically. "I know you won't. How could you? Just look at her!"

They both did. Like a Broadway star responding to her cue, Jane rose to the occasion. She opened her mouth wide. She stretched up her arms and splayed her little, dimpled fingers. She made her absolute best speech. "Ahhh! Da!" And then she beamed with delight at her own performance.

"Oh! Oh!" Allie said brokenly, tears streaming down her cheeks. She snatched at the baby and pulled her close. "Oh, you darling, darling gorgeous girl! You precious thing!"

"She's just herself, isn't she?" Connor said. "She's not anybody else. Some people don't realize that about babies. Maybe it isn't obvious until you've spent time with them. They're not made up of other people's bits. Their mom's hair and their dad's nose. Grandma's stubbornness and grandpa's tendency to snore. They're just themselves, and it takes no time at all until you love them purely for that.''

Allie didn't answer him, and he didn't seem to expect her to. He just sat back on the couch and watched her as she held Jane for several minutes in silence. Finally she said, "How can I, Connor? How can I take her back?"

"Karen's said it's okay, you told me."

"I know, yes, but I don't know what I'm doing. Karen has been her mom since her birth. What if changing Jane's universe like that damages her in some way? What if Karen can't deal with it, after all? She loves Jane as much as I do. For Karen to lose her now…"

"What? Are you planning to spirit her off to the other side of the world, or something?" Connor teased. "Jane and Karen are never going to see each other again?"

"No, of course not!"

"Then do you have to deal with those details now?" he pointed out. "You've made a decision. A huge one. Isn't that enough for today? There can be some kind of transition. You have options. Work it out later."

She let out an enormous sigh. The universe shifted. A suffocating weight seemed to lift from her chest. "You're right." She paused, testing the idea in her mind, then said simply, "Thanks. Thank you. I really mean that."

"Helps to have the perspective of someone who's not involved, sometimes," he told her.

Connor heard the gruffness and reluctance in his voice. Those words hadn't tasted quite right. *Not involved.* He was starting to have the strongest inkling that he *was* involved, that he had become far more deeply drawn into the lives of A. J. Todd and her baby daughter than he'd have thought possible in a mere twenty-four hours.

And he didn't want that. Not one bit. Not with the way he'd been feeling lately.

Look at those huge eyes of hers. She was staring in his direction but he could tell she wasn't even seeing him. She was looking at the pictures made by her imagination, sifting them through in her mind, as if sifting through a set of photos, deciding which ones to keep and which to discard.

There was something about her, a combination of strength and vulnerability that tore at his heart. He felt he already knew her the way he knew his brothers, to the point where he could pull apart the things she did and understand each separate strand of behavior and motivation. He sensed that she was tough about a lot of things, could imagine her coming up with her plan to be a radio announcer—then going at it for all she was worth.

Somewhere in her past, there had to be some great scene where she'd stormed into some station manager's office with her demo tape and demanded to be given a hearing. She'd probably won the guy over with thirty seconds of that liquid, honey-rich, teasing voice of hers. He wished he'd been there!

He was sure that she would tackle whatever challenges came her way with a unique blend of fairness, stubbornness and tact, and emerge stronger after every bucket of icy water that Fate tossed in her face.

But what had actually happened to her had been a very different sort of crisis, a personal drama of violation, loss of control and emotional conflict that was sourced in the very center of everything that mattered to a human being. For someone like Allie, that was a whole lot harder to deal with. What had happened to her wasn't something that responded to her usual tactics. Instead, it needed intuition and a faith in her own heart that she was struggling to find.

He felt a huge, almost irresistible need to step in and help her with it.

But he was well aware of how restless he'd been lately. He'd been experiencing a familiar sense that something was missing, that he had needs, and things to prove to himself, that weren't getting filled in his life as it stood. In the past, this sense had sent him catapulting out of the warm bonds of his extended Philadelphia family and into a series of far-flung and quintessentially male adventures. Stunt work, oil drilling, roadying.

If he did blow off the commitment he'd made to Patrick and Tom's software company, what could he put in its place? What would top those outrageous career episodes? Lion taming in a circus, perhaps? Looking for buried treasure?

Yeah, right!

None of it appealed. Neither did some far more practical types of employment than those. He'd been there. He'd done that. He'd lived those itinerant, men-only life-styles. Bunking down in cheap motels or crowded staff quarters. Eating junk food like there was a ten-million-ton meteor about to slam into the earth the day after tomorrow. Did he really want to go back to any of that? No way!

Yet the restlessness remained, the sense of something missing. He was happy working with his brothers, so he didn't truly think it was that. He couldn't put a finger on it. It wasn't quite the same feeling as it had been in the past, he decided. If anything, though, it was stronger.

And one thing he was sure of. It meant that any kind of an involvement with Allie was out of the question. At the best of times, she wasn't the kind of woman who invited or deserved the love-'em-and-leave-'em treatment. And for her, right now, this very definitely *wasn't* the best of times.

As Karen had warned him very clearly, she'd been through a rough patch, and it wasn't over yet. Something in her poignant situation cried out to him for his help and support, but feeling the way he did, he knew it would be totally unfair of him to start giving it to her.

Totally unfair.

Which meant that he had to ignore the way his body responded every time she moved. He had to ignore the way his hand itched to reach out and touch her hair, the way he couldn't get the image of her wet body out of his mind. Every inch of her skin had been so taut and smooth. Her dripping, transparent cream underwear had been tinted a delicious rose where her nipples had puckered against the fabric of her bra. His fingers had been as disciplined as good little soldiers as he'd pulled the clothing from her body, but he knew he would be haunted by fantasies of what those fingers could have done if he'd been stripping her for another reason, with her feverish encouragement.

He stirred and stretched, and knew quite well why every muscle and joint in his body felt so stiff. It was nothing to do with the physical exertion of dragging Allie from the lake and carrying her to the house. Nothing to do with the ebbing pain in his leg. It was the fight going on between his brain and his treacherous male hormones that was making him ache like this.

"You didn't finish your soup," he said to her, breaking the silence and standing up, badly needing a change of mood.

"No, I...got distracted."

"It's okay. I'd like to get something more substantial into you, anyhow. It's almost three o'clock."

"No! You mean we've been talking since—"

"Yep. Couple of hours. I'm going to fix us some burgers and give this little lady a late lunch." Jane had been getting bored for the past ten minutes, and was starting to fuss.

"I can do that," she told him. "I'm warm now. I feel good."

Physically drained, though, he guessed, watching her scramble to her feet. It hadn't hit her yet—probably she still had adrenaline burning in her system after what she'd been through, physically and emotionally, today—but he knew it would. At some point in the next few hours, she'd go out like a light. Before that happened, he needed to get some more food into her.

So they spent the next hour in a repeat of yesterday evening, all three of them in the warm kitchen while Jane got mashed fruit and custard all over her face, and the smell of sizzling burgers filled the air. After her meal, Jane was ready for another short nap, so Connor took her upstairs and sang her off to sleep in her little blue crib, because he knew that Allie would fall asleep, too, if she got within six feet of a bed, and she hadn't eaten yet. Then they both ate their burgers and oven fries at the kitchen table, and drank long glasses of soda.

At seven, after Jane had awoken, played for a couple of hours, had another bottle then gone off for the night, Karen called on her cell phone with the latest report on her situation.

"The minivan's at the repair shop. I'm feeling okay about driving. I've picked up the rental car and it's fine. I tried to call around noon, and a couple of times after that, but you let the machine pick up. I guess you guys were out playing in the snow."

"Something like that," Connor told her. He wasn't going to scare her with the story of Allie's plunge through the ice.

"How come you didn't call me back? I was starting to get a little worried."

"Sorry, Karen, things got busy and we forgot to check the machine." He'd actually turned the sound down while he and Allie were talking.

"Busy?"

"I'll tell you later."

"How's Jane?"

"Gorgeous. Asleep." He hesitated for a moment, then decided he might as well be blunt. "But, Karen, if your hidden agenda for this weekend was getting Allie to recognize that she wants her daughter back, then I think you've succeeded," he told her.

Karen gasped. "Connor, what happened?"

"What had to happen eventually," he said. "She realized that the way Jane was conceived didn't make one bit of difference to how much she loved her."

"She *told* you? *That's* why you weren't picking up?"

"Yeah, she told me. Almost all of it, I think. About your pregnancy, too. Congratulations!"

"Thanks. We're over the moon about it." Her voice softened briefly. "But, darn it, Connor, what's been going on? Can I speak to her?"

"She's in the bathroom right now. We've just eaten some supper. I'll get her to call you back."

"Actually, maybe not," Karen said slowly. "Maybe not. I don't think I want to deal with this over the phone. The last thing I want is to push."

"Makes sense," he agreed.

He put down the phone a minute later, and when

Allie appeared and he told her Karen had just called he wasn't surprised when she said, "I'm not going to call her back, unless she needs me to. I—I'm not ready to talk about this yet."

So he put on some music and revived the dying fire. Then he stood behind her as she sat on the couch and massaged her aching shoulder and neck muscles, strained from clinging to the sled this morning and hauling herself onto the ice. He'd only meant to do it for a few minutes, but it felt good and right, so he continued until she admitted in a blurred voice, "I'm almost asleep."

"It's what you need," he said, coming around the couch and looking down into her sleepy eyes. "You should go to bed. Can you make it upstairs on your own?"

"I'd better," she joked. "Having you carry me twice in one day would be setting too much of a precedent."

"Dangerous things, precedents," he agreed.

She didn't answer, but they both felt the danger, and the awareness, vibrating between them like the lingering twang of a guitar string, holding its place in the air for far longer than seemed possible.

He let her go, and then heard the sound of the shower running upstairs, her footsteps as she moved around her room, and finally silence. He waited until he was sure she'd be asleep, then put on his coat and hat and gloves, and went outside to start up the snowmobile. He spent the next hour going up and down the track between the lake and Mason Hill Road in the chilly darkness, using the noisy machine to tamp down the powdery snow in case Karen made it through tonight.

As a variant on the old cold-shower routine, it was almost as useless in getting rid of unsated desire, but at least it fulfilled another more practical purpose.

"It's okay, Allie, I've got her."

"Karen! You made it back last night!" Allie said in a creaky voice.

It was almost seven in the morning, and she'd awoken automatically at the sound of Jane's crying and headed through the connecting door to the other bedroom. Jane had slept for twelve hours, and Allie herself must have had almost eleven.

"About eleven-thirty, midnight," Karen confirmed.

She was busy as she spoke. She picked Jane up out of her crib, then made a face at the wet patch on the back of Jane's stretchy pink sleep suit. The diaper had leaked. It didn't faze Karen. She'd obviously dealt with it a dozen times before.

Hardly needing to think about what she was doing, she spread a change pad on the bed, grabbed a clean outfit from her suitcase, pulled the pink suit's snaps undone and slid it off. Jane's flailing arms and exuberant legs were only a momentary inconvenience.

In contrast, Allie would still have been struggling clumsily, terrified of giving a painful twist to one of those darling little limbs out of sheer inexperience.

Meanwhile, Karen still managed to both coo and

gurgle at Jane, *and* carry on a self-mocking narrative about her saga of disaster yesterday.

Her competence daunted Allie. A stranger would have had no hesitation in identifying Karen as the mother and Allie as the childless aunt. She couldn't stop the self-doubting thoughts. *Can I really do this? Is it right? It's certainly not going to be easy....*

There was a movement in the doorway, and there stood Connor, dressed in his usual jeans and dark sweatshirt. He must have been fresh out of the shower, because his hair still curled damply on his lean, strong neck and his face was newly shaved. His aura of energy overflowed the door frame and half filled the room.

As he stood there, he offered a casual, "Hi," and his eyes flicked from Allie to Karen and Jane and back again, taking in the scene.

Allie flinched.

"I slept for eleven hours. I can't believe it," she said, although this wasn't remotely what concerned her at the moment.

Connor knew it, too. She could tell from the waves of expression in his face—the little frown between his brows as he watched Karen snap up the fresh outfit across Jane's chest, the way he opened his mouth as if to speak, then shut it again, the veiled yet searching look he shot back at Allie.

Are you okay about this? it said.

And it said something else, too, something that had her body suddenly tingling and her arms folding self-consciously over her chest. Lace-edged flannel pajamas with a pattern of small blue flowers weren't exactly the most seductive fashion in nightwear, but they were capable of giving away far too much about the body beneath, all the same.

Why did she respond to him like this, when every rational—and terrified—cell in her brain told her not to?

"Pancakes or waffles?" he asked.

"Gee, you really believe in breakfast, don't you?" she exclaimed. The everyday subject of food was a relief. "I still haven't recovered from that half pound of bacon I ate twenty-four hours ago."

"Got to build up your strength after yesterday," he told her.

But that got Karen curious. "Yesterday?" She frowned, then solved the problem to her own satisfaction. "Oh, right. You were taking pictures in the snow. Thank goodness we won't need those now!"

"I love your faith in our total incompetence," Connor said.

"Am I wrong?"

"On the contrary, Karen, you are *so-o-o* right!" Allie put in. "We were a disaster."

"Oh, I don't know…" Connor defended their efforts with a drawl. "I reckon there's one or two shots that might have been worth something."

Allie caught the hot glint in his eye and had to beat back a flush by sheer force of will.

"I doubt it," Karen said. "So let's eat and get on with it."

She picked Jane up off the bed, threw her into the air and kissed her with a loud smacking sound on her cheek. Jane loved it, and Allie felt winded.

*I'm jealous. Of my own sister, with my own baby.
I hate this!*

She drew in a ragged breath, and Karen must have
heard it. She turned in Allie's direction, with a hor-
rified expression that she hastily tried to hide. Connor watched the two of them for another second,
then disappeared. Allie knew perfectly well that he'd
deliberately left them alone to sort things out.

"Allie, I'm sorry," Karen breathed, giving up on
the pretence that this wasn't happening. "I've hurt
you. You had Jane for a whole day yesterday, and
you did just great with her. Now I've just barged in
and claimed her as if none of that counted."

"It's okay."

"No, it's not. I'm running on my nerves. I'm not
thinking. I'm really, really sorry."

"Please don't make a big deal out of it." She
meant it, and Karen recognized that she did. The
last thing Jane needed was to have her mother and
her aunt in conflict over her.

"Sure," Karen said carefully. "Sure, Allie."

Very slowly, she held out the baby and Allie took
her, swallowing the lump in her throat. "Hi, Janey,"
she said, holding her close, and then led the way
down the stairs.

Chapter Six

"Okay, now, Connor, you're leaning on the ax and you're looking at Allie and the baby," Karen commanded from behind her camera. "You're concerned about them. Remember, this woman and her child have been in a war zone. She's buried two brothers and a husband, and there's some mystery about the baby and about her."

"Got it," Connor said.

"You're not quite convinced that she's who she says she is. Allie, you're thinking about what you've been through. You don't know that he's watching you, and you're wondering if you dare to tell him the truth. No, like I said before, don't pull faces like that. Just try and think into how she'd be feeling and the expression will come on its own. Okay, that's much better. That's great! You guys are starting to relax a bit."

"Did I ever say I thought this would be fun?" Connor growled. "I hadn't realized models worked so hard! After today, I'd say it's right up there with brain surgery and preschool teaching as far as heavy input goes."

"All right, now, costume change!" Karen ordered several minutes later. "We're done with the exteriors. I'm going to use that fireplace."

"Will it look right?" Allie asked. "Isn't it meant to be a tiny little cabin in the woods?"

"Yeah, but I can change the detail, remember," Karen said. "I just need the look of the flames and what the firelight does to the light and shadow on your faces."

It took an hour to get the fire right, as well as their indoor costumes. Then Jane needed a nap and Allie assumed they'd have to stop, until Karen announced, "Not a problem. I want just the two of you now. This is much later in the book. Grab that gun, Allie. Yes, I know it looks plastic, but it won't when I paint the scene. Now, you've told him the truth about your husband, Allie, and even though the two of you should be enemies, you can't resist how you feel about each other."

"I beg your pardon?" Allie didn't manage to keep the alarm out of her voice.

Karen didn't trouble to repeat her statement. "Clinch time," she ordered briskly.

"But you said to pick up the gun."

"I know. And you're holding it to his chest," Karen explained patiently. "But it's obvious he's about to kiss you. Or, in fact, you're about to kiss him. It's actually the heroine, Savannah, who makes the moves. She's the one with all the experience, remember. The hero, Brady, is a virgin.''

"I am?'' said Connor weakly.

"Today you are,'' Karen replied.

"I don't think you explained that point when you told me the plot of this thing.''

"And I don't want to know how big an imaginative leap that is for you, Connor. Just make it, okay?''

Karen took the trouble to glare at him for a whole quarter of a second before returning to her relentless professional pace.

"Gun three inches higher, Allie. Connor, don't look frightened. She may be the one taking the lead, but in fact she's a lot more scared than you are, and you're all man, even though you haven't seen another human being in six months.''

"Right,'' they both said to Karen at once.

Gun at Connor's chest. Clutched in both hands.

"Your hands look shaky. That's great,'' Karen said.

Connor's face was inches away. Clearly, he was wasted as a computer-gaming expert, Allie decided. He should have dropped the film stunt work and gone straight into Hollywood male leads. How did he manage to convey the idea that this was what he most wanted and what he most dreaded, at the same time? Allie felt her lungs shrink to about one quarter of normal capacity.

"Go for the lips, Allie,'' Karen ordered.

"I just love the sensitive wording of your instructions, Sis," Allie answered, and moved her face an inch closer to Connor's. Reluctantly.

"Not close enough," Karen said.

"Should I move?" Connor wanted to know.

"No, you stay right where you are," Karen said. "You're perfect. Allie, *please*..."

"Okay!" She jerked her head forward and felt as if she were being bathed in the light of his eyes.

"Great! Half an inch is what I want."

It's not what I want, Allie thought desperately. It's about six feet too close.

"Great shoulders!" Karen said, clicking away.

The shoulders were bare, and the tawdry pink satin dress was a size too big. Karen said she'd change the color when she painted the scene, and it was good that the size was wrong. It added to Allie's aura of vulnerability, the way it slipped down her arms, and was perfect for the character.

"Okay, now, hold her, Connor."

"My dress is falling off..."

"Connor, hold it up."

More rapid clicking. Allie felt Connor's fingers on the bare skin of her shoulders, and the fan of her own breath against her bottom lip, coming much too frequently.

"Lean over a little, Allie. And back again." Click, click, click. "No, that's wrong, isn't it? Try resting the gun on his shoulder, pointing at his neck. Close your eyes. Connor, try grabbing the gun, but almost as if it was a part of Allie that you really like. Now kiss him."

"Um..."

"Please..." Karen begged.

"What the heck, Allie, let's get it over with," Connor growled. And his mouth came down on hers before she could say another word.

For once, Karen didn't say anything, and even the clicking of the camera seemed quieter and less obtrusive. Allie closed her eyes and forgot about the gun resting on Connor's shoulder, even though it still weighed in her hand. All she could feel were Connor's fingers closed warm and firm over her knuckles, and his mouth softly tasting hers, his thighs slipping against the satin of the dress and his other arm pressing against her back.

His lips were tentative at first. He was holding back, a little self-conscious, just as Allie was. But then that gradually evaporated, like fog on a winter morning, and left only sensation. His mouth was firm, warm, smooth. His long lashes tickled her cheeks as he broke contact for just an instant and moved his head to the side. Allie's bottom lip trembled and dropped open as she let out a slow gasp and then a jerky sigh.

When they surfaced, Karen had a complicated look on her face—satisfaction mixed with slightly awed surprise—and she was about five feet from the camera.

"Out of film," she said, then gave a somewhat goofy grin. "But that's okay. I'd say we're done."

Connor scratched his head and stepped back a pace. He looked dazed, and he was frowning. "Were we any good, do you think?"

"Oh, you were great. You were amazing."

"So you don't need us to do…any of it…again?" Could that be a note of regret in his voice?

"Hope not," Karen said. "Before we came up here, I was fully intending to go with an exterior scene, because it gave the flavor of the wilderness that's so crucial in the book. The gun scene in front of the firelight was just a bonus, just in case. But I think I'm actually starting to like it best. Or even…let me think."

She grabbed the pencil and pad that she kept by her while she worked and scribbled down some ideas, illustrated by sketchy lines and shapes that didn't make any sense to Allie.

Actually, nothing made sense to Allie right now. She was still overwhelmed by the power of Connor's kiss. She knew that, like her, he hadn't wanted to do it. Despite their combined will, however, the kiss had taken control of both of them, had acquired a life of its own.

They shared the same reason for their initial reluctance. The kiss mattered. It was important. It was the crystallization of everything she had begun to feel about him. A trust and a connection deeper than she'd have thought possible in so short a time. A stirring of the senses that told her she hadn't lost her ability to feel that chemistry for a man, even though the thought of going any further with it still panicked her terribly. A sense of promise, as if the kiss was only the beginning.

And no kiss ought to have that power, especially over a woman who was at such a vital crossroads in her life. A man like Connor, with everything going for him, didn't need to get involved in any way with a woman like her.

"I can hear Jane," Karen said, breaking off from her feverish sketching. "Do you want to get her, Allie?"

"I—actually, you can, Karen, if you don't mind. I have a question I need to ask Connor."

"Sure." With unusual obedience, Karen hurried up the stairs, and Allie scarcely waited until her sister had disappeared before turning fiercely to the tormentor at her side.

"Are you crazy?"

"I'm starting to wonder..."

"You are crazy! Why did you kiss me like that, as if it was real?"

"Because it was."

"I—no, it can't be. That would be—"

"Hey," he protested, "I'm simply reporting the facts. Tell me I'm wrong. Tell me it wasn't real for you, too."

"I...can't tell you that."

"Didn't think so."

"Don't sound so—so—" she accused helplessly.

"So what?"

"Grim."

"I'm just agreeing with you. And I agree with what you're going to say next, too."

"What am I going to say next?"

"That we're going to pretend it never happened. That our timing makes the Titanic and the iceberg look like a piece of precision planning. That there are more questions hanging over your life than there are mosquitoes over a Minnesota pond in June. That getting involved with a man is about as high on your agenda as going for another fully clothed swim in that lake out there. Isn't that what you were going to say next?''

"No," she said flatly, "because I couldn't drum up that level of fluency in a month of Sundays. Not when my emotions are running this high. But it's what I would have meant, if you'd let me stumble through it."

"Good. We're in complete agreement. Because the timing is a total disaster for me, too. That makes things easier."

"What 'things'?"

He shrugged. "Just have a feeling…"

Allie did, too.

Karen came downstairs with Jane, who had a red crease mark from her sheet pressed into her cheek and tears in her eyes. She wasn't properly awake. Allie wanted to take her and lay her head against her shoulder and kiss away the tangles of grumpiness and sleep. But, as usual, Jane looked so right in Karen's arms.

Allie had to physically force herself not to reach out for her baby.

"Did he answer it?" Karen said.

"Did who answer what?" Allie frowned.

"Connor. Your question."

"Oh." She shot a look in Connor's direction and flushed. "Yeah, I guess he did. With bells and whistles."

There was a tiny silence. Karen just nodded.

"We should grab some lunch, then start to pack up if we want to get back to Philly at a decent hour," Connor said, gruff and businesslike.

It was like an ice-hard snowball hitting Allie in the chest with perfect aim, and it winded her just as badly.

"Already?" she bleated in a panicky voice.

"We have to return the rental car to the airport, and that'll probably add an hour to the trip," he pointed out. "I'm assuming the three of you will hitch a ride back with me."

"It's not a problem, is it, Connor?" Karen asked.

"Not at all, but we should get on with it. Don't you think?" He was talking to Karen, but looking at Allie.

"Yes. Of course. I was forgetting about the rental car," Allie said lamely.

So much had happened in this isolated place in just a day and a half. It was like being in one of those old-fashioned little glass snowstorm toys, a separate, magical world of its own. In contrast, Philadelphia was reality, and the place where the new step she had decided on in her life would have to begin.

I'm not ready. Not to do it. Not even to tell Karen.

Connor seemed to be able to read her mind. "Karen, Allie has something she wants to talk to you about before we start packing."

Connor, I swear, I'm going to put my hand over your mouth in a minute...or stick a fistful of snow into it, if that's what it takes.

He didn't flinch at the furious, terrified look she

gave him, and didn't let her get away with the emphatic shake of her head. "Not now."

"Now, Allie," he commanded gently. "Don't you think she knows anyway?"

"Of course I know," Karen said. "I knew it before we even came up here."

"Then you planned—" she began in an accusing tone.

"Didn't plan, Allie. Just knew it with a mother's heart. You want her back."

Allie let out a trembly sigh. Karen did know. That made it just a little easier.

"So badly!" she admitted to her sister. "Can't believe it's so strong! But I don't know how to do it, Karen. I mean..." She laughed, mocking her own helplessness, even as she felt her eyes fill with tears. "Do you remember how hard it was when Aunt Sue gave Mom and Dad her cat? He ran forty blocks to his old home five times before he got settled with them. Oh, I'm crazy, comparing a cat to my baby, but—"

"Do you think I haven't thought about this, Allie?" Karen said. She handed Jane to Connor without even looking at him and took Allie in her arms. Her body was soft and warm and sisterly in the loose pink sweatshirt she wore. "You're not simply going to take Jane back to your place with her crib and her diaper bag, like taking a kitten home from the pet store."

"I guess not, but..."

"Of course you're not! You're going to move in with John and me for as long as it takes."

"With you and John," Allie echoed.

It felt like the perfect transition in her growing relationship with Jane, but she was all too aware that Connor lived right next door. Having him that close was a complication she already didn't need.

Chapter Seven

"Next up, forty minutes of your favorite country songs from the eighties, nineties and beyond, back-to-back, here on WPYR. We Play Your Requests. Nonstop Music, Nonstop Stars."

"Well, get on with it, then," Connor growled at the male announcer who was filling his car with sound.

He didn't want to hear this guy. He wanted to hear Allie. Unfortunately, she didn't work the evening drive-time program, and right now he was on his way home from work at the end of a long day. Maybe he wouldn't mind this guy so much if he had a decent chance of seeing Allie herself when he got home, but the possibility was slim. She had been living at her sister's, right next door to his own place, for eleven days now, and they hadn't set eyes on each other.

Why did he have a problem with that? he asked himself as he changed lanes and then saw the red glow of brake lights just ahead. Wasn't it what he'd already decided was for the best?

But he knew the answer already.

Every step in his thought processes was one he'd covered a hundred times already this week.

She doesn't need me. She has the baby to think about, and the changes that will make to her world. I don't need her. I've got to work out what's eating at me about my life first. The fact that I can't stop thinking about her is exactly why I'm not going to call or go over. The fact that she hasn't called or come over shows that she knows it would be a disaster, too. We agreed on that. I'm a rational man. I know what's good for me, and I'm completely capable of acting on that knowledge.

So why did his heart do a back flip when he turned into his driveway and saw what was happening in the driveway next door?

Karen's husband John was loading two suitcases into the trunk of a taxi, parked beside the paved path that led up to the front porch. Bundled up in a big red coat, Karen was sliding into the cab's rear seat, and it didn't take much in the way of deduction to work out that the two of them were going away for a long weekend.

Without Jane?

Connor checked. *No baby. No baby gear. Definitely without Jane.*

The taxi pulled out of the driveway. Karen caught sight of him and waved, her smile not quite reaching her eyes. He knew this was a brave step for all three of them—Karen, John and Allie—to acknowledge that the baby belonged to Allie now. John was a quiet man, steady, with the capacity to be a devoted father. Giving Jane back to her biological mother would be tough on him, too. No doubt the weekend away had been deliberately planned as part of the transition.

Connor waved back to Karen, his mind already bursting with wild plans that he wasn't going to act on. Of course he wasn't going to rush over there with a big bunch of roses and sweep mother and child out to Philly's finest restaurant for a candlelit dinner for three.

The idea was tempting, though. So tempting, in fact, that when he got inside his house, picked up the phone, dialed his trusty pizza-delivery service and was asked for his order, he heard himself saying, "Two large, please. One anchovy and black olive, and one mushroom and onion."

They'd eaten pizza on the way home from Diamond Lake eleven days ago. He could still remember Allie's catlike table manners. How did a woman manage to eat pizza that neatly, yet with that much enthusiasm for the taste of it? The combination ought to be impossible. He now discovered that, along with memories of her tongue flicking at a misbehaving string of cheese and her white teeth nibbling at the crunchy crust, he'd filed away in his brain the information that mushroom and onion were her favorite toppings.

The pizza place must have been busy, because he

had exactly twenty-nine minutes in which to regret his double order. He made good use of those minutes, and by the time his doorbell rang, he'd decided to eat the second pie tomorrow for breakfast. He was pretty fond of mushroom-and-onion pizza himself.

Allie probably didn't need him, and definitely didn't want him. He had managed to steer clear of her for eleven days, turning down a dinner invitation from matchmaking Karen last weekend with the truthful claim of a prior commitment at his brother Patrick's. No sense in undoing all that hard work now, just because Allie and Jane were alone.

So he ate the anchovy-and-olive pizza on his own. He chased it down with a beer, and channel-surfed with the remote until his eyes hurt and his brain was crowded with confused images of tennis players serving to hockey goalkeepers, and French actors making love to news reporters.

Upstairs, looking for something a little more constructive to do, he suddenly saw her. She was twenty feet away, pacing back and forth in the room she now shared with Jane. On previous evenings, the room's drapes had been closed, but tonight they were open. The room was brightly lit, and Jane was crying.

A lot.

Connor could tell from Allie's face that the baby must have been crying for a while. He couldn't believe how quickly she'd taken on the look and gestures of a mother—the same ones he'd seen on the women in his extended family all his life. The way they tilted their chins downward to look at their baby's little face, so close to their own. The patient, tender, simmering sort of expression they wore as they patted and crooned and soothed.

He saw Allie offer Jane a bottle, but the baby screwed up her little pink mouth and turned her head away. Then he saw Jane pulling and scrabbling at her left ear, which gave him an inkling about what might be wrong.

Enough spying, he decided. It wasn't his style. *Enough staying away.* He was going over there. Which didn't mean he was in any way getting involved, of course. Allie needed him, that was all.

He arrived about forty seconds after the pizza guy, and had time to see Allie awkwardly juggling cash, crying baby and two large pizza boxes. Connor and the delivery guy crossed paths on the front steps. Allie had seen him coming and was waiting in the doorway.

"Hi," he said.

"Karen and John have gone away for the weekend," she told him.

She didn't waste words on formally inviting him into the spacious hallway, just stepped back, let him through, then shut the door behind him.

Her face was tight and upset now. "I'm sorry, Connor. Can you take these?" She practically threw the pizza boxes at him, and he caught them. "I'm so distracted…"

"Do you think she could have an ear infection?" he asked.

"Oh, is that what it is?" The relief vibrated in

her rich, husky voice. "She's been crying since before they left. We thought it was just because she had a late nap and woke up grumpy. I told them to go and not even think about it, but that was an hour and a half ago. She was fine this afternoon. I kept thinking she'd stop. I ordered these pizzas. Then I got worried. Do ear infections come on that quickly?"

"Don't know. I think they can. But she was pulling at it, I noticed, and that can be a sign."

"You *noticed?*"

"Through the window. You left the drapes open," he explained.

"Is that why you came over?" Her dark eyes met his for a moment, then slid away before he could interpret their expression.

No, it isn't, he wanted to say.

To hell with not getting involved!

That's the excuse for why I came over. I care about Jane and her ear, but I care more about you. Does that make me a heel or a hero?

Instead of admitting the truth, which would probably have made her even more uncomfortable than it made him, he said, "Do you have the phone number of her pediatrician? I think we should see if they're still open, or we'll have to go to the emergency room."

"Karen left the number by the phone. I'll call now. I'd just about gotten to that point anyway, even though I didn't know what could be wrong. She feels warm, doesn't she?"

He came closer and felt the baby's forehead with

the palm of his hand. It did feel warm. Though possibly not as warm as *he* felt, all over, with his shoulder brushing against Allie's. She was too distracted to notice.

He took the baby from her while she made the call, watching the way her expression changed, the way her pretty mouth moved, listening to the different emotions in her voice. She ended by saying, "Oh, you are? You can? Right away? That's great!"

Putting down the phone, she told him, "Dr. Seiken was just finishing up, but he's going to wait for us if we come straight over."

He loved the way she just assumed he was coming too, although she hadn't even realized that was what she was doing. And he had to smile just a little at the way she couldn't start the car in the cold evening air because she was so jittery and impatient. Jane was still crying, and Allie was ragged at every nerve.

"Would you like me to do it?" he finally offered.

"I'm fine."

And she was, eventually, after she'd flooded the engine with gasoline by pumping too much on the accelerator, and had had to wait for it to drain again before she started it successfully.

Halfway down the street, as the car's motion soothed Jane into silence at last, he asked, "So, you know where this place is, right?"

That drew a blank stare from those big eyes, followed by a hollow-voiced announcement. "We'll have to go back and look it up."

"No, we won't. I have my cell phone right here.

I'll call Dad. He's been practicing family medicine in this city for thirty years. He'll know.''

Connor punched in the number and got his father on the fourth ring. ''Dad, can you tell me where the pediatric practice of...?'' He turned to Allie with the question in his face.

''Seiken, Marshall and Chung,'' she supplied.

''...Seiken, Marshall and Chung is located? Somewhere along Seventh? Okay.''

''Seventh and Greenwillow, I remember now,'' Allie said, nodding.

''Thanks, Dad,'' he said into the phone. ''No, it's not important. I'll tell you later.''

''Thanks, Connor,'' Allie echoed.

''I can be useful, sometimes.''

She gave him another blank look as she waited at the lights. Her mouth dropped open. ''Connor, why are you here?''

She was talking half to herself. He just grinned at her, and waited for the self-recrimination. It came.

''Oh, glory! I just roped you into spending the best part of your evening on this, didn't I? Without even saying please?''

''Did I object?''

''No! You're too well brought up.''

''I'll pass that on to my mother.'' He grinned. ''She'll be astonished but grateful.''

''Don't tease! I'm too embarrassed. I—that second pizza was for you. I was going to ask you over, anyway. To thank you—''

He groaned. ''Alison Jane Todd, can you please *stop* thanking me?''

"—for everything that happened up at Diamond Lake. And I had thought you might like to know that things are going well with Jane. My first weekend with her, just me. Only of course now they're *not*..." Going well, he understood, though she was too churned up to say it properly. "Because she has this ear infection. If that's what it is."

"And it's your fault, right?" he teased.

"She had a cold earlier in the week. Maybe I should have—"

"Most babies get ear infections, Allie."

Ten minutes later, Dr. Seiken told her the same thing, after he'd confirmed the diagnosis by peering into both the baby's ears and her throat, and listening to her chest as well. No chest or throat infection, but Jane's left ear was good and red inside, and she'd need a course of antibiotics and some painkillers for the first day or two.

He seemed like a caring doctor, about the same age as Connor's dad. He wrote out a prescription and gave them some instructions, and the only difficult part about the whole thing was that he seemed to assume that Connor was Jane's father, and that he and Allie were married.

Connor almost laughed aloud at the sight of Allie trying to choke back a convoluted explanation of the truth, then he gave in to a wicked impulse and said to her, as he dropped a supportive arm around her angora-clad shoulder, "Let's go get that prescription filled, sweetheart. I'm sure Dr. Seiken wants to get on home."

Allie bottled up her response to this until they

reached the car. Then she exploded in an indignant froth of questions. "Why did you do that? Act as if we were married?"

He shrugged. "He seemed to expect it. That stuff he was saying about new parents...I take it he hasn't met Karen or John?"

"No, they started out with another practice and weren't happy with them, so they switched. In this practice, I think they've only seen Dr. Marshall. I didn't want to go into the whole, complicated story, but maybe I should have done."

They lapsed into silence. In the backseat, Jane was fretting again. They stopped at the pharmacy to get the prescription filled. By the time they got home, she was exhausted and ready for bed. So Allie and Connor rather clumsily got the antibiotic and the painkiller into her mouth using the plastic droppers provided for each, and then Allie took her upstairs for diaper change, bottle and bed.

Connor prowled. He considered just letting himself out the front door and going back home, but there in the kitchen sat those two pizza boxes, hastily dumped, and he knew he wasn't going to be able to pass up the chance to spend the evening with Allie. His resistance to what sparked between them seemed to be zero.

"Anchovy and olive," she announced to him when she came down, indicating the pizzas.

All was silent upstairs, and he didn't need to ask if Jane was asleep. The anxiety had dropped out of Allie's face, leaving it tired but filled with that unique contentment and relief he'd seen in mothers before. Baby asleep. All's right with the world.

"That's your favorite, isn't it?" she added. "I remembered. I'm sorry it's gotten so late. You must be starved!"

He wasn't, of course. Far from it. He'd already consumed an entire olive-and-anchovy pizza at home. But he didn't tell her that. It was well worth enduring the penance of eating another one, he'd already realized, in return for spending more time in Allie's company.

Who knew where it might end? his body said. His mind, at the same time, fought a losing battle for control....

Why did I think this was a good idea? Allie asked herself as they ate their pizza together. *I should have known it would be like this. So perfect. Just him and me, with Jane asleep upstairs, and music playing, and so many things we keep finding to talk about.*

And the only thing worse than the talking is the silences, because then I feel my head pulled like a magnet to look at him, and when I do, I discover that he's looking back at me. But then he flicks his eyes down, and pretends he's looking at his pizza, and all I can see is those eyelashes of his. And it's unfair that any man should ever have eyelashes that long and that thick and that kissable. Help! Have I ever thought about kissing a man's eyelashes before?

"I guess you have your program to do in the

morning?'' Connor said, when the pizza had disappeared, and coffee and cookies as well.

They were sprawled on separate couches, set at right angles to each other, with a glass-topped coffee table between, in Karen and John's bright-yet-cozy living room. There was instrumental music in the background, and they had been talking, traveling the whole world in the course of a single conversation.

Allie's mind was so far away from the day-to-day that she didn't even understand him at first.

''My—Oh, yes! What's tomorrow? Friday? Yes, I do. So of course I should get an early night, and—''

''I think you've already missed the boat on that one,'' he said on a drawl. ''It's ten after eleven.''

''I'm going to be a mess in the morning,'' she muttered.

''Tell me about it!''

''You don't have to wake up at four-thirty!''

''No, but I haven't gotten to sleep yet, and I have an idea I'm not going to for quite a while,'' he drawled, lazily sweeping the room with his eyes before staring deliberately at her.

''No?'' she said.

''No. And do you need me to tell you why?''

He was coming over to her, stretching his hands out to pull her to her feet. Allie let him, not because he hadn't given her a choice, but because the need in both of them was so obvious and so strong. She melted at his touch, sang inside at the way his blue eyes fixed on her, challenging her to read him the way he was reading her.

They didn't kiss. That was the incredible part, Allie thought. They simply stood there, hands joined, then wrapped around each other, and looked. But it was more powerful than any kiss she'd ever had. The feel of his warm palms closed over her knuckles and fingers, then pressed against her sides. Those blue eyes of his like a sparkling ocean she could almost have dived into.

"What are we going to do about this, Allie?" he finally said, rocking her slightly in his arms.

"Make it go away." Because the panic was still there, almost as strong as the need.

"How?"

"Do I have to come up with all the answers?" she said shakily.

"Hey, I still haven't worked out all the questions yet!"

"What have you got so far?"

"Well, for a start there's, 'Where am I going with my life?' That's a biggie. Then there's, 'Is it fair to take anyone with me?' Actually, I have the answer to that one. It isn't. Hell, I can't get involved with you, Allie! We've both known that from the start. The timing is too wrong. For both of us."

"Worse for me," she said. "I haven't figured out half of what I need to about becoming a mom. How can I start to think about becoming a lover? I can't!" She didn't fully admit to her terror at the very idea.

"I know. I understand that," he said. "It's like we're holding hands across a chasm and neither of us knows how to get across. That chasm is trying to tell us something, I guess. I shouldn't have come tonight.''

"No," she agreed. "But I'm glad you did. For Jane's sake," she added. It didn't convince either of them.

"Arghh!" he growled. He broke their contact and wheeled away from her, pressing his palms against the sides of his head, leaving her immediately cold despite the warmth of the room. "So am I! Go to bed. Do your program. Have you got anything on for the weekend?''

"Just Jane and me. Might drive up to Allentown on Sunday and have lunch with my parents. There's a couple of friends I could call. I've got some catching up to do with them.''

"They don't know yet that Jane is yours? No one does?''

She ticked off on her fingers. "Karen and John and my parents know, of course. One friend, also in Allentown. The others here in Philly? Not yet. And I'm not sure if I'm quite ready to tell them.''

"When do Karen and John get back?''

"Sunday night. John has a conference in Orlando tomorrow. The rest of the time they're goofing off. It was kind of hard for them to accept that they could do that. Or that they should. But they need it.''

"So do you," he answered. "Don't go to your parents', or see your friends. Spend the weekend with me instead.''

"Connor—''

"I know. I know." His voice was so strident with

frustration that it hurt his throat. "But I can't let it go yet, Allie. I can't! Even if that means the whole thing has to explode in our faces first. And can you honestly tell me it's any different for you?"

She looked at his blazing eyes, his hair all thick and wild on top of his head, the way he held his hands as if they tingled with the need to touch her.

"No," she said. "I can't."

Chapter Eight

"Stay with us here on WPYR," Allie said. "This hour and throughout the day that stands for We Play Your Requests. Just call us and ask. If you're in the bath, in the car, eating your cereal or still in bed. Call us! Next up, this hour's most requested song, and if you requested it, you go into our draw for—"

The prize. Oh, lord, she'd forgotten this week's prize. Was it a set of CDs? Dinner for two? A sound system? Her open, frozen mouth turned into a yawn and her producer, Charlene Taylor, quickly cued in the next track and saved her skin.

"The trip, Allie," she chanted. "The weekend for two in Nashville, remember?"

"Right," Allie nodded. "The trip. I'll apologize for the technical glitch and repeat it after the song."

"You have it written right there."

"I know. I froze."

"You look exhausted."

"Stayed up late."

"Bad girl."

If you knew! And I have a horrible feeling I'm going to be a lot worse!

"I'll grab you another coffee," Charlene promised.

The coffee, as thick as shoe polish, got Allie through the last half hour of the program, but it meant she drove home jittery and tense. Jane was at home with the baby-sitter Karen had been using for the past six months, an older woman called Hope, whom Allie was starting to like as much as Karen did.

When Allie had listed to Connor last night the people who knew the truth about Jane, she'd forgotten Hope, and she felt bad about that. Hope was one of the people who was making this transition possible.

"She woke up about an hour ago," Hope reported, rinsing some dishes in the sink as she spoke. Her chunky, grandmotherly hands were clad in pink rubber gloves. Jane was sitting up in her playpen with some toys, and Hope had a CD of children's songs playing in the background. "She's just finished her cereal, and she had her medicine. That painkiller must be working, because she's not showing any sign of the infection bothering her. But you look exhausted. Want me to stay on while you take a nap?"

"No, I'll be fine," Allie insisted.

As soon as Hope left, she called Connor at home,

knowing she'd get his machine, and told his recorded voice, "I'm going to cancel the weekend, Connor, if that's okay. I'm too tired."

Too scared, also, but she didn't admit to that.

When she'd finished the call, she felt so much better that she was able to bundle Jane up in a snowsuit and blankets and take her for a long walk in the stroller. Then, after baby food and canned soup for lunch, they were both ready for a long nap. Allie slept the sleep of the just and innocent, curled up on the couch downstairs, until she was woken by an impatient hammering at the door.

It was Connor, who evidently didn't check his machine very often.

"Oh, I checked it all right," he said, standing on the doorstep, with his hands in his pockets and his shoulders padded by a chunky brown bomber jacket. "You reneged."

"No, I came to my senses," she corrected.

"Well, I haven't, yet," he said, "And I left work early especially."

She relented, opened the door to let him in, and wondered why relenting felt so nice. It shouldn't. She ought to be spitting mad at the way he wouldn't take no for an answer. Problem was, most of her brain and all of her body wouldn't take no for an answer, either, even while butterflies of panic flitted around in her gut.

"Jane's asleep," she informed him.

"We'll wait till she wakes up, then."

"Wait for what?"

"To go to the mall."

"The mall?"

Suddenly he turned thoughtful, reflective. "Yeah, I know," he said, prowling around Karen and John's comfortable blue-and-yellow living room with his big thumbs hooked in the front pockets of his jeans. "I wondered about that, too."

He'd shrugged off his jacket, and now his flannel shirtsleeves were rolled to the elbows and the front of the shirt was unbuttoned far enough to show a triangle of bright white T-shirt at the neck.

"Kind of suburban, isn't it?" he went on. "Tame. Feel like I should be taking you horseback riding, or snowboarding, or something. But that wouldn't work with Jane, and anyhow, I don't feel like this is going to be tame. I feel like it's going to be an adventure. Weird! I never go to malls!"

"Then I guess that does make it an adventure," she agreed. She couldn't help smiling a little as she watched him. "I mean, it all comes down to what you're used to, doesn't it? It's what you make of it. If you grew up in a South American jungle, a mall would be an adventure. And if you don't keep your eyes and your ears and your heart and your mind open to life, to all its huge moments and its tiny ones, then nothing is an adventure."

He looked at her. "Is that what it is? I think you're right." He repeated the words even more thoughtfully. "I think you're right."

And he looked so awed by whatever calculations were going on inside his head that she said to him in a joking tone, "Cost you fifty dollars, those words of wisdom."

"I'll pay it, too," he said. "Worth every penny."

Then he laughed, as if to shrug the whole thing off, and a few minutes later Jane woke up and they took her in Allie's little royal-blue car to the mall, where they window-shopped and tried out some toys, bought a xylophone on wheels and a blue dress for Jane for next summer, ate an early dinner at the food court, window-shopped some more and finally went to a movie, which Jane slept all the way through.

"So how did it rate for you?" Connor asked in the car on the way home.

"The movie? It was great!"

"No, I meant the total mall experience. Was it an adventure?"

Allie thought about it as she drove. "I guess it was, in a lot of ways," she said. "It's the longest outing I've done with Jane. The first toy and the first outfit I've bought for her. I hadn't dared to before. Just the thought of it made me...made me..."

"You don't have to explain."

"I poured everything into making the quilt for her, and that was hard enough." She changed the subject quickly, still aching about the six months with Jane that she'd lost, even while she didn't know how it could have been any different. "What about you, Connor? Was it an adventure for you?"

"Yeah, scaling the mighty escalators. Battling with the plastic alligator rocker. Exploring the uncharted territory on Level Three. Sampling the exotic native cuisine." He grinned.

"Didn't we agree before that—?"

"Oh, you want the serious answer!"

"Actually, yes."

"Okay." He gave it to her, staring ahead at the road and speaking slowly as she studied his profile in snatches when she could take her attention from her driving.

"It was fun," he said. "A heck of a lot more fun than sitting over too many beers with a whole lot of guys who don't have much of any depth to say even when they're sober, let alone when they're drunk. A heck of a lot more fun than jumping off of a fake burning building for the seventh time in two hours. The adventure part was in there, too, somewhere. I know it was. But I haven't figured out where, or why. Can I get back to you on that?"

"Any time," she told him, and spent the rest of the journey regretting how much of an invitation there had been in those two simple words.

Saturday was one of those unseasonably mild days that February in the Northeast can suddenly throw at you.

"Days like this make me go a little crazy," Connor told Allie at ten in the morning when he appeared at her front door with a bunch of daffodils. He was in short sleeves.

"Me, too," she answered, trying not to notice what his white T-shirt did to the outline of his upper arms and the contours of his chest muscles. "These are gorgeous, Connor. You didn't get them from your garden?"

She bent her head to brush the cool yellow trumpets of the flowers against her nose.

"No. I have some coming up, but they're not out yet. Is Jane awake?"

Allie cocked her ear toward the stairs behind her. "How does that sound?"

There was a happy, high-pitched singing noise coming from the upper floor.

"Yeah, I'd have to agree that's awake. Great. I was hoping she would be. The two of you want to come to the park with me and watch ice melt?"

"Um..."

"Before you answer, I should warn you, in case you didn't catch the forecast, that it's supposed to snap back to eighteen degrees tomorrow."

"Really? Eighteen?"

"Maximum. With snow overnight."

"Actually snow?"

"Whereas it's supposed to hit seventy today. By the feel of the sun on my back a minute ago, all warm and soft, I reckon it could squeak to seventy-two."

"I'm sold," Allie said, laughing. "Let's go watch ice melt."

It was great to be able to take Jane out in the fresh air in nothing but a pink playsuit and a purple spring jacket. They took Allie's car and drove to a wild piece of park near Connor's parents' house, where he'd played as a child. Allie was astonished when he unloaded a packed picnic basket.

"You really planned this!"

"I planned the event," he corrected. "Took me,

oh, about forty-five seconds when I went out to pick up the newspaper this morning and felt the air. The gourmet picnic hamper company planned the menu.''

They put Jane in her stroller, and Allie wheeled it while Connor took the basket. When they'd reached a secluded picnic bench, they parked Jane in the sun to watch them, and left the picnic hamper and the diaper bag to keep each other company. Then they both went crazy with the warmth and sun and air, and jumped on frozen puddles for the sheer pleasure of seeing the ice shatter, threw soggy snow-balls at trees till their bare, wet hands were red and turned their faces into the sun and closed their eyes just to soak up the light.

''I can feel that vitamin D,'' Connor crooned. ''Ooh, it's good!''

Jane took a bottle in her stroller and fell asleep, so Connor and Allie ate their picnic a little early, their appetites sharpened by the exercise and the fabulous air. Then they walked and talked, pushing the stroller, until Jane woke up and drew their attention, in a not very subtle way, to the fact that Allie had forgotten to put any actual diapers in the diaper bag she'd so carefully brought with her.

''I can't believe this!'' she wailed.

Connor was laughing.

''It's not funny!'' She glared at him. ''We'd better get home.''

''Guess we had,'' he agreed, still looking more amused than anything else.

''Why can't you stop laughing?''

"Because it's great, Allie. It's wonderful. You know what it says to me? It says you're a real mom now."

"It does?" she squeaked. "Oh, Lord. Just the opposite, I would have thought."

"No, because in my extensive experience, this is what happens to real moms all the time," he insisted. "My sister-in-law, Julie. My other sister-in-law, Meg. My cousins. They bring three kinds of baby food and forget the spoon. They wipe the baby's face so carefully, and don't notice there's a big smear of pureed plum on their own blouse."

"They lug this great, bursting diaper bag round with them for the entire morning and half the afternoon, and there's no diaper in it?" she suggested with some skepticism.

"Happens to a mom or a dad somewhere in the world approximately every nine minutes," he assured her solemnly as they began to walk back toward the parking lot. "Tell me, though, Allie. Isn't it true? Aren't you starting to feel like a real mom?"

Suddenly, he wasn't laughing and he wasn't teasing her, and she knew that his question was serious. He came closer and dropped an arm around her shoulders. It felt so right that she couldn't help nestling her head against his upper arm. His touch invited her to share what she felt.

She took a big breath. "Actually, I am feeling that way." She paused and thought. "It's weird. It's incredible. It's still less than two weeks since I decided to do this...to try it. I was so scared of it, had no confidence at all...wondering what it would do to my feelings about my career. But already I can't imagine what it would be like...can't remember what it *was* like...not to have her. It feels like I've been doing this forever. There are no issues with my work, other than being a little tired.

"I thought I'd be scared when I woke up yesterday morning. No Karen. Just me and Jane and a little snatch of Hope for the whole weekend. But I wasn't scared at all. Karen's called twice, and the second time I almost told her, 'Enjoy your marriage, give yourself a break, and don't keep pestering me with your calls! Jane and I are doing just fine.'"

"So I guess you'll be ready for the next step pretty soon," he suggested. "Moving back to your place."

She frowned and started to ease away from him. His fingers trailed down her bare arm as if inviting her back soon. The effect of his touch lingered for a long time, fuzzy and tingly and good.

"Don't know about that," she said. "I think I'll be okay about it in another week or two. But I know it's going to be harder for Karen than she's letting on. John, too. It was a lot harder for them to leave this weekend than it was for me to be all by myself with Jane. You know, it's like mother love operates on a one-way switch. Real easy to turn on, impossible to turn off. My apartment's over an hour's drive from Karen and John's place when there's traffic. I wish I lived closer."

They reached the car. The parking lot that adjoined the park was crowded now, and puddled with melting snow. Connor watched as Allie deftly maneuvered the stroller wheels around the puddles and parked Jane by the car's rear door.

She pointed her bunch of keys at the vehicle, pressed a button, and the car gave an electronic yelp as its doors automatically unlocked. Allie was a small, highly efficient whirlwind over the next minute. Door open. Stroller straps unfastened. Jane buckled into her car seat on top of a layer of paper napkins left over from the picnic.

Stroller folded. Trunk opened. Stroller and picnic hamper and uselessly crammed diaper bag tossed inside.

Only then did she stop long enough to look at Connor, who was standing there watching. She grinned. "It's good, Connor," she said. "Apart from the distance issue with my apartment, it's *really* good!"

He nodded. Didn't need her to explain anymore about what she meant.

"That's great, Allie," he said, and wondered about the huskiness in his voice.

Wondered for a whole ten seconds before it hit him, as he watched her standing there in the parking lot, still grinning at him, with the puddles and the grass and the trees all glistening around her, her strong slim legs in their blue jeans anchored slightly apart, her dark hair scraped up into a careless ponytail, and the sun already turning the skin on her bare shoulders, above her periwinkle-blue T-shirt, to pale honey…

She was the reason for the restlessness inside of him. It was impossible, because he'd felt the restlessness before he'd ever met her. But it was true, all the same. His soul had been yearning for a new adventure, a new landscape, and the adventure was a woman like Allie.

Not a woman like the ones he'd met in the course of his here-today-gone-tomorrow life over the past ten years—women who hung out in dreary bars or worked in scrape-by jobs, women who blew in and out of a string of relationships like a carnival ride blowing in and out of a string of county fairs.

He'd been afraid to get involved with Allie at first, because he didn't feel he could guarantee that he wouldn't blow in and out of her life in that same way, but now he knew he'd been wrong. He was ready. He didn't want to leave his brothers' company. He was happy there. *This* was the new adventure he'd been craving for in his life, something far deeper and more enduring than all the ones he'd tried before.

Allie slid into the driver's seat, and he took the passenger seat beside her. As on yesterday's trip to the mall, they had taken her car because it had been easier than moving Jane's car seat from one vehicle to another. He loved the slightly erratic way she drove. Today, with all his perceptions heightened and his mind sharpened by revelation, he saw something symbolic about it. When it came to the pace and nature of their relationship, Allie was the one at the wheel.

What they had…what they were just beginning to have…was still as fragile as the ice they'd shattered so joyfully today, as fragile as the more sinister ice she'd fallen through two weeks ago. She'd told him today that she'd had a couple of nightmares about that. Mixed-up, action-filled scenarios in which her fall through the ice was confused with even darker images of loss and violation.

He had no illusions that this relationship was going to be any smoother than Allie's driving. She loved her baby and was learning how to raise her, but he sensed there were things she hadn't worked through yet about what had happened to her, things she would have to work through some day soon, although maybe she didn't even realize it. Until that happened, he'd just have to go along for the ride.

"Connor, help, is it left here? Or right?" she demanded suddenly. "I've forgotten."

"Left. Then right at the next light," he told her, and once again the symbolism of it struck him. He was navigating, telling Allie where to go next. Did that apply just to this short car ride? Or did it apply to their lives as well? He had the idea, growing stronger inside him each moment, that it probably did.

"You're eating at my place tonight, right?" Connor said to Allie over the phone.

They had said goodbye to each other as soon as they reached home, about, oh, half a minute ago. For some reason, he'd called her the moment they were each inside their respective doors.

"I am?" she answered him. "Connor, I—"

"You definitely are. I'm sorry. I forgot to clarify that earlier. I'll see you at six."

He put down the phone before she could say anything more, and she just had to shake her head. For about the twentieth time today, he'd brought a goofy sort of grin to her face and a warm, achy sort of feeling to her heart. She didn't know whether to make a huge effort and drum up some anger or simply admit to herself straight out that she wasn't angry at him, she was happy.

Actually happy.

And still scared.

She and Jane spent the rest of the afternoon quietly, then went to Connor's at six and found him cooking up a storm, with the smells of garlic and spices and seafood filling the house and spilling through the open kitchen window.

Allie hadn't been to his place before, but she immediately felt at home there. Like Karen and John's, it was a generous-size, high-ceiling Victorian home. Connor was partway through restoring it, in an irreverent way that worked surprisingly well. She didn't know what the original owners would have thought about the large new opening from the upper floor to the front hallway, and through the hall floor down to the basement, but she liked the added sense of space and light as much as she liked the bright, unusual colors of the ceiling trim, door frames and skirtings.

"What's cooking, Connor? It smells fabulous!" She had already sat Jane on the square of kilim carpet in Connor's dining room with a couple of toys she'd brought with her.

"Paella," he said. "Not that I'm trying to impress you or anything."

Then he grinned, and she grinned back, caught too quickly by his mood to do anything else. It was scary and wonderful and...

No, mainly it was scary, she revised. He *was* trying to impress her, and he didn't mind one little bit about letting her know it.

"You never told me you could cook," she said in a feeble voice. "Even when I admitted that I couldn't."

He shrugged and grinned. "Anyhow, my repertoire is extremely limited, although it's amazing what ten years of lousy meals at bad restaurants will do to your motivation. This is the splashy little number I always whip up to dazzle a lady friend. It kind of segues right into the black satin sheets and the vintage Doors album on the surround sound."

"You have black satin—"

"No," he interrupted patiently. "I don't have black satin sheets. I don't have surround sound, either. Didn't want to scare you off, so I thought I'd go lateral and try some humor."

"I'm sorry..."

"No, *I'm* sorry. Rest assured, my intentions are really, really evil, but at least they have the virtue of being announced right up front."

"How evil is evil?" Allie asked. "Since we're being up-front."

It was pointless to act surprised or coy about this. She had known why he was asking her over. Heck, they were both adults, with a chemistry like nuclear fission glowing between them, stronger every time they met and every time they touched. She'd had the whole afternoon to say no. And she hadn't said it. She ought to be honest with herself about why that was. It didn't mean this was easy. It didn't mean they'd be able to make it work. She had huge doubts, *huge*....

He put down the wooden spoon he'd been using to stir the paella and came over to where she stood, just inside the doorway of his sleek, newly modernized kitchen.

"Oh, I'd say just a little bit more evil than this," he said softly, and pulled her into his arms as if he were gathering up a huge bunch of flowers.

Then he kissed her. Hard. With exuberance. At length. His mouth was electric in its confidence and expertise, but it didn't feel like a planned demonstration. She could sense the emotion behind it, and when she let her eyes drift open for an instant and saw that his were closed, as if he were seeing deep into some other world, she knew that he was as lost in this as she was.

"Oh, Allie...mmm, Allie," he muttered, as if he hardly knew he was speaking at all.

His tongue traced the line of her lips, then parted them to enter her mouth. His palms grazed her breasts, with a featherlight pressure that teased her nipples instantly to hardened peaks. He dropped his hands to her waist and bracketed them around her hips, pulling her against him so that they fit like puzzle pieces, then he brushed his body a little to the side, as if he understood how much time she needed, how slowly she needed to go.

Slowly…slowly was heaven. There was time for her to fully experience every tiny moment of touch, every nuance of pressure and sensation. Time for her to accept the intensity of her response and of his need.

It felt so fabulous, all of it, that she was quite breathless by the time he finished. He let her go gently, slowly, watching her with a smile that softened his eyes and mouth and betrayed his satisfaction. She felt hot and swollen and melting, and impatient for the chance to respond more fully, more deeply, more nakedly. She also felt even more terrified than before. Not about what had just happened, but about where he would expect it to go next. Sure, he'd been joking about the black satin sheets, but…

Suddenly she shivered and hugged her arms across her front.

I'm not ready for this.

She began to distrust his stated honesty. What did that mean? Wasn't it just another male tactic, not a whole lot better than Jerry Purcell's tactic of crying on her shoulder and drugging her coffee? Wasn't it just an excuse to bulldoze this chemistry between them through to its logical and most physical conclusion?

Bed.

She didn't want that. She'd never opted for casual relationships in her life, and she was even less inclined to do so after what had happened to her fifteen months ago, and now that there was Jane. When a woman was a mother, she didn't just have her own needs—her own blocks?—to consider. She had to consider the needs of her child, and children needed stability, people in their life that they could count on.

"Don't, Connor," she told him, her voice dark and shaky.

"You don't want dessert before the main course, huh?" he teased on a whisper.

"I don't want dessert at all."

"Funny. I got the impression just now that you had a pretty sweet tooth." She saw him step back to study her new stiff, protective stance. His eyes were narrowed and thoughtful, despite the teasing drawl.

And she'd had enough of their flirting humor. "Stop playing games with words, Connor. We talked about this up at the lake, didn't we? It's not going to work. We agreed on that."

"I'm seeing things differently now."

"Well, I'm not!"

He was silent for a minute, then, "Did you bring some food for Jane?"

"Yes, but I think I should—"

"Go?" he interrupted, getting to the heart of it at once, as always. "And waste this? You're not going, Allie. You don't need to. I'm not the kind of guy who can't hear what a woman is really saying."

"No?"

"No. I understand, okay? You're not ready."

"Or maybe I don't want it at all."

There was a beat of silence. "Maybe you don't. I'm not pushing. So stay. No strings."

Allie had no reason to doubt him, and every reason to doubt herself. She knew her reactions weren't as consistent and healthy as they should be at this point in her life. So, against the clamorings of panic and doubt inside her, she stayed, ate the best paella she'd ever tasted and wasn't nearly as relieved as she should have been when he said good-night at the end of the evening without so much as the ghost of a kiss.

Chapter Nine

"**S**he loves it, she loves it, she loves it," Karen chanted gleefully.

She had just put down the phone in the office-cum-studio she had created out of what had once been the formal living room of this substantial old home. Now, she was dancing into the kitchen, where Allie had Jane in her high chair eating her evening meal.

"Who loves what?" Allie said.

"Nancy Sherlock loves my cover."

Allie let out a squeal. "That's great, Karen!"

"Isn't it? I spoke with the creative director at her publisher, who said they'll definitely want me to do more work for them."

"Which version did they go with?"

"Both."

"Both?"

"The fire scene's going to be on the inner cover, and the snow scene on the outer. You know, ice, fire. Their initial distrust of each other, the heat of their passion within. Great symbolism."

"Does that mean we get to see it now?"

"Sure." Karen had superstitiously refused to let either Connor, Allie or John look at the progress of her cover design until she knew whether it would be accepted. Now, basking in the glow of its success, she seemed eager for them all to see it at once, if not sooner.

"Damn!" she said. "John's not getting home till late. Check Connor's house, Allie. Are there lights on?"

Allie stood up, taking Jane's rubber-tipped spoon with her, and peered through the kitchen's side window across to Connor's place, just as a light went on, and then another. "Looks as if he's just got in."

"I'll call him." Karen punched in the number and Allie went on feeding Jane, wishing too late that she hadn't admitted to seeing those lights next door.

She had seen him a couple of times since Saturday, each time for only a few minutes. On Monday night he'd dropped in to borrow a video Karen had promised him. On Wednesday morning he'd just been heading out in the company of his older brother Patrick, both dressed in expensive suits, when Allie was coming home from the radio station at a little after ten.

"He's coming right over," Karen said happily when she put down the phone.

"Great!" said Allie with false enthusiasm.

He arrived within five minutes, dressed as he had been yesterday in a dark gray business suit with co-ordinating shirt and tie. Allie thought about all the different kinds of clothing she'd seen him in thus far and wondered if there was any kind of outfit that *didn't* make Connor Callahan look like the most gorgeous hunk of manhood any female could ever hope to meet.

Just looking at him made a part of her want to run her hands over that suit to see how it felt beneath her fingers, slide the jacket off his shoulders, loosen the tie and...

Then the other part of her took over. Freeze. Flashback. Dread. Doubt.

A familiar progression of feelings. She kept coming up against this wall, and didn't want to think about what it meant. *Not yet. Not yet.*

Think about Karen's cover art instead.

Karen had gone to her office and brought it out, carefully protected by a thin cardboard folder. Now she was holding it, waiting for the perfect moment to unveil it.

"It's enlarged," she explained. "They'll reduce it when they print it. And of course it still needs some of the detail. The blurb on the back, et cetera."

"Are you nervous, Karen?" Connor teased. "Nancy Sherlock loved it, remember. Our opinion isn't worth squat against that, is it?"

"I didn't think it would be," Karen admitted, too nervous to mask the truth. "But I'm discovering that it is. Your opinion is worth a lot. You're the models, and I kind of sense that the way you both—'' She broke off. ''Look, Allie, just don't shriek, okay?''

''Okay,'' Allie promised.

Karen laid the folder down on the kitchen table and opened it with one quick movement, spreading the two pictures out so that they were side by side. Then she darted back to give them a clear view, and bit her bottom lip hard.

So did Allie, purely in order to stifle that shriek she'd promised not to let out. Enlarged to four times the book's finished size, the pictures looked bright and bold and passionate, dominating the mood of the cozy, family-style kitchen.

Although Connor and Allie were both recognizably themselves, the intimacy of their expressions and the drama of their poses had been deftly heightened by Karen's skilful brushwork and her dramatic use of color—the cold, glittering blues and whites of the snow and winter sky in a mountain landscape, followed by the flame and golden wood tones of a fire-lit log cabin.

In the first picture, Connor and Allie…or Brady and Savannah, as they had now become…had their gazes locked on each other, each with pupils dilated. Jane, dressed as Savannah's boy baby, Will, stared directly out from the picture with a haunting self-possession, despite the innocent chubby cheeks and swaddled limbs.

In the second picture, the gun on Connor's shoulder, pointed dangerously at his neck, jarred in an intriguing way with the sensual suggestion of their imminent kiss. Allie said somewhat shakily to

Karen, "Nancy is right. It makes me *instantly* want to read the book, Karen. A gun, a baby, that desolate cabin, and those two passionate, haunted people. They're not us anymore."

"But they are," Karen said. "The photos came out even better than I thought, even the ones..." She hesitated and looked a little shamefaced. "The ones you took with Connor's disposable camera," she finished in a rush. "Would you believe the expressions on your faces in the snow picture I got directly from one of the photos you took? I mean, the light and the framing was terrible, but—"

"If it makes you feel better to believe that, go ahead," Connor told her kindly. "I have no ego attachment to this process. I'm just a natural photographic genius, that's all."

It broke the odd tension that had grown up in the kitchen, and all three of them laughed.

"So, may I use the two of you again, for the next runaway bestseller I'm bound to be asked to do? Probably, oh, next week?" Karen asked, her nonchalance a transparent veneer over her visible sense of achievement.

"No!" Connor and Allie spoke in unison almost before she'd finished.

"Oh, guys...why not?" Karen wailed in a pleading voice.

Jane chose the moment to protest loudly against being ignored.

With burning cheeks, Allie grabbed the spoon again and began to feed Jane some fruit puree. She choked and spluttered. Allie apologized to her.

Karen grabbed a spare bib and wiped up the mess, as if afraid that splatters of it might fly through the air from the high chair to the table and damage the precious cover art.

The issue of Connor and Allie working on a repeat performance as models was forgotten.

For the moment.

At Karen's insistence, Connor stayed to eat, his suit jacket tossed onto the sofa in the living room, his tie stuffed into a pocket and his shirtsleeves rolled. He didn't seem in any hurry to leave. He was still there when Allie came down from putting Jane to bed, by which time John had arrived home, had been pounced on by his eager wife, and was being given a detailed report on the success of the cover art and a private viewing of it in Karen's studio-office.

"Coffee?" Connor asked Allie.

"No, thanks. It'll keep me awake," she hedged.

"We never answered Karen's question, did we?"

"Which question?" She remembered as she said it.

Why had she reacted as if she'd been stung when Karen suggested modeling with Connor again?

"Yeah…that question," he said to her. "We both said no. Do you think we'd both give her the same answer as to why?"

"Is it important?"

"Might be," he answered. "I'm still thinking about it."

"Let me know when you come up with a theory," she said. The lightness in her tone wasn't genuine.

She was on edge now, and getting more so by the minute.

"I will," Connor said. "Believe me, you'll be the first to know."

You're wrong, she wanted to tell him three weeks later. *It's becoming more and more obvious that I'm already the last to know, when it comes to what's happening around here.*

A lot had happened in three weeks. There was a warm, important sense inside her that there had never been a time before she was Jane's mother—in every way—and this sense had become stronger and deeper in Allie than ever.

Karen, meantime, was learning to let go—not of her love for Jane, which would always be strong and true, but of her feeling that Jane belonged to her. She trusted Allie's decisions now.

She was approaching the three-month point in her own pregnancy, and the baby inside her was becoming more and more real and significant. The severe nausea that had so often gripped her over the past six weeks was just beginning to taper off, and she, John and Allie had agreed that when it was gone, it would be time for Allie and Jane to go back home.

In many ways, Allie was looking forward to that final transition, but she had a nagging certainty that she should be looking forward to it a whole lot more. For a start, it would make Karen's relentless yet apparently oh-so-casual plotting and planning a lot harder to carry out. Her interfering big-sister agenda was sticking out a mile, and if Connor wasn't actually a part of the conspiracy, he sure seemed more than happy to go along for the ride.

By the time Karen crossed into the calmer waters of the second trimester of her pregnancy, however, she wasn't bothering to use any excuses at all.

"Since you're moving back into your place on the weekend, Allie, I thought we should get Hope to sit for us and all go out to dinner to celebrate."

And just who, exactly, was "all"? Allie didn't have to ask. She knew that Connor was included.

She wasn't surprised when Karen told her to "dress up special," in her best little black dress. She wasn't surprised when the restaurant turned out to be one of the most expensive in the area. She wasn't even surprised when Karen suddenly appeared to crash after her entree, denied any interest in dessert and claimed only that she needed John to take her home at once to bed.

"But you two stay," she suggested generously.

"Do we need your permission, Sis?" Allie said in her best radio voice.

Karen deliberately misunderstood the gentle jibe. "No, of course you don't, Allie," she cooed. "Enjoy yourselves here until the place closes."

John tried to hide a smile behind his blunt hand. Lord, yes, he was in on it, too! And she'd always thought he was such a trustworthy, sensible type. A minute later, the two of them had disappeared.

"One of the things I love most about my big sister," Allie said through gritted teeth and a sweet little smile, "Is how wonderfully subtle she is!"

"It's a great quality," Connor agreed.

Allie scowled.

"Hey," he protested softly. "Is this so bad? We've seen a fair bit of each other lately, but none of it has been what you'd call intimate."

"No?" she challenged, then immediately regretted it.

After all, he was right. She hadn't been alone with him in more than three weeks. So why did she have a dozen memories of moments that seemed as intimate as could be?

The time he'd held out her coat for her to put on, and she'd felt his fingers gently loosening and lifting the hair from inside her collar. The time Jane had thrown a spoonful of food in his face, and Allie had suddenly found herself practically falling into his lap as she apologized and fussed with a wad of tissues and wiped at his cheek, almost losing herself in the deep, steady blue of his gaze. The time he spent a half hour entertaining Jane with bouncy rhymes on his knee while Allie folded laundry and John and Karen cooked pancakes and they all drank coffee.

Some of those memories felt as personal and private as if they'd been alone together on a desert island...or an island in the mountains, surrounded by a frozen lake.

"No, Allie," he insisted. "As far as that goes, spending time together when it's just us, this relationship is going nowhere."

"Relationship? We don't have a relationship," she snapped in a panicky tone.

"Not for lack of trying, at least by certain people."

"I'm sorry. I truly am. It's embarrassing. I'll tell Karen—"

"Don't. Please."

He stretched his arm across the table and trapped her hand beneath his. She flinched. But it felt so good. How could it make her feel so wonderful and so frightened at the same time?

"There's only one thing I want you to tell Karen," he went on. His blue eyes were like faceted jewels, and his lower lip was full and sober. "And that's, thank you for your efforts at matchmaking. They've been entirely successful."

"Connor—"

"Don't tell me I'm pushing. I'm not. You're ready for this now. Don't you want it as much as I do?"

She snatched her hand away. "I thought you said...you've said all along that you didn't want it. That it was the last thing you needed in your life."

"Can't a red-blooded man change his mind?"

"But I haven't changed mine," she insisted wildly. "I—I felt safe when you were saying that there was no future to the chemistry we had. And didn't you say to me a few weeks ago that you knew how to listen to what a woman was really saying?"

"I do. I believe I do." He leaned forward across the small table until he could almost have kissed her there and then, if she had leaned forward too. She didn't move an inch. She couldn't take her eyes off his lips, his dark, dilated pupils.

"You *are* saying that you want this," he told her, "Sure, not with words, but with every movement your body makes when I'm around, every look you give me. Every time we laugh together. Every time your face lights up when you tell me something cute that Jane did. You want this. And yet whenever there's a chance we might be alone, when we might get somewhere with what's happening, you sabotage it.

"Like the other day when John and Karen went up to bed, and you followed hard on their heels thirty seconds later. Like two weeks ago, when you brought my vacuum cleaner back and I offered you coffee and you told me Jane needed a nap, when I knew she was happy with Karen."

"So listen to that," she said her voice low and stormy. "Take notice of that. Take notice of *this*. My leaving this restaurant. Right now!"

She didn't trouble to hide the fact that she was acting out of sheer terror. Instead, she broke their hypnotic eye contact, slid to her feet, grabbed her bag and fled, forgetting until she reached the restaurant's chilly parking lot that she'd come in Karen and John's car.

She was still standing there on the steps, steaming breath heaving in and out, too upset to go back into the restaurant and call a cab, when Connor caught up to her.

"Need a ride?" He ran a hand from her shoulder to her hip and then let it drop.

"No."

"Oh, come on, Allie...."

"Well, yes, I need one, but I don't want one. Not from you. I'm fine. Don't you think it's better if we keep out of each other's way for a while?" It sounded like a plea, and it was.

"So you can cement those emotional blocks of yours a little more firmly in place?"

"Emotional blocks?"

"Yes! The ones you need to accept and start working through before this thing between us can go any further."

"How can you speak with that degree of authority about what's going on inside of me? What gives you that knowledge? What gives you that right!"

He gripped her arms, then slid his hands upward until he reached her neck. He stared down into her face as he smoothed her hair back and softly tangled it in his fingers.

"Because I *care* about you! How many ways do I have to say it? No, I didn't want to. For quite a while I didn't want to care about you at all. I was restless, wasn't sure that I knew where my life was headed. I did know that I needed some kind of adventure. We've talked about this. Then I realized. This is the adventure. This!"

He bent his head and brushed a hot, quick kiss onto her mouth. It was the first time he'd kissed her since that night at his place when he'd cooked paella for her. Desire surged inside her like a jet of hot liquid, then softened into a sweet heaviness.

"I knew you needed time," he said. "I know you still do. But please at least admit that we share a goal."

"We don't. I—I won't admit that."

Deliberately, she made her body stiffen. But she

didn't have to fight him off. He could sense the determined stubbornness of her withdrawal and stepped back a pace, his shoulders tight and hunched.

Stubbornness. It was a quality Allie could reach for inside herself when she needed it. She had done so before. It hadn't been easy, several years ago, to convince the station manager at WPYR that a liquid voice and an enthusiasm for country music made up for a lack of broadcasting experience. She had a college degree, but that was in music, not communications, and the station manager had dismissed the value of it completely.

But she had been stubborn. She'd made the best demo tape she could and taught herself about radio by working the graveyard shift at a tiny public broadcasting station that folded after a year. Then, at last, WPYR had hired her.

And if the same stubbornness and persistence was required to convince Connor that, for whatever reason...she wasn't going to give him a reason, reasons weren't important, she thought wildly...to convince him that she *didn't want* this, then she'd use it.

"We don't share a goal about this, Connor," she repeated. "I don't want it. It's simple—no, it's not, I guess," she corrected herself. "The chemistry's there. That's a complication. But chemistry is no foundation for anything."

"There's a lot more than chemistry."

"Sure. We could have been friends, if you'd wanted that."

"Friends?" He laughed, and it came out like a cynical yell. "Does that ever work?"

"Okay, not friends." She gave a deliberate shrug. "Suits me. We can get out of each other's lives completely. Best thing for everyone."

"Allie, is this fair? This denial?"

"Fair to who? You, I suppose. And *denial* is a loaded word."

"No, fair to *you*. And denial is what's happening. This isn't about us, it's about Jerry Purcell, and I can understand—"

"You understand nothing." Suddenly, she was shaking, her voice so tight and hard it hurt. "Nothing, Connor Callahan."

"Have you thought that he might be doing to other women what he did to you? Tricking them? Manipulating them?"

"I'm not going to talk about this. I'm not going to think about it. I have enough other things to deal with in my life."

He went on as if she hadn't spoken. "Have you thought that maybe you owe it to yourself, and Karen and John, and, yes, even me, to track him down and confront him? Or go to the police. Or get some counseling, talk it through with a professional. Or *something,* so that you can move forward. It's still inside you, Allie."

"Enough!" She knew that the color had drained from her face, but the strength hadn't. She glared at him, scowled, spat sparks with her eyes. "Get out of my face, Connor. I'm thinking about Jane, not Jerry. That's past. That's irrelevant. And you need to just...just...get out of my face, okay? Stop pushing! I'm calling a cab and I'm going home.''

"Okay, Allie." All at once, he sounded tired. "Okay, you win."

She watched him, expecting more, but there wasn't more. Again, with even more weariness in his voice, he said, "You win." Then he loped off the curb and wove his way through the parking lot to his car.

She watched until he was out of sight before she went back into the restaurant to call a cab, and she told herself very firmly that she hadn't been hoping he would turn around and come back. *Never. No way. Not at all.*

Chapter Ten

Connor did it systematically. It was tempting to go the other route, just pick up the phone and start calling every Purcell in the Philadelphia telephone directory, or radio stations all over the United States at random. But he curbed his emotions and forced himself to take the approach that would reap results.

Logic. Strategy. The same skills the people in the Games Division at Callahan Systems used when developing and testing a new software product.

Accordingly, on the morning that Allie and Karen and John spent moving Allie and Jane's things over to Allie's apartment, Connor ignored the activity next door and sat down at the computer in his study at home. He used the Internet to generate a list of all the radio stations in the Northeast that would be big enough to employ someone with Jerry's technical qualifications. It made sense to start in the

Northeast, and he could expand the search farther afield if necessary.

It also made sense to start with country music stations, but there, when he started calling, he drew a blank. He widened his search to include rock, rap, jazz, classical, talk radio, news radio and sports radio, and over the next week got sick of the sound of his own voice uttering the words, "May I please speak with Jerry Purcell?" to more station receptionists than he kept a count of. Philadelphia, Trenton, Baltimore, Pittsburgh...

Why am I doing this?

The bleakness of mid-March mocked his efforts, and when Karen and John invited him over for pizza on Thursday night, there was a hollowness at the heart of their jokey conversation. Allie wasn't there. He heard a detailed report on her and Jane. Both doing great. Allie had already started looking for a closer apartment. She also wanted something that was near a park with a playground, for when Jane got a little older.

"But...you haven't seen her, Connor?" Karen asked with a frown.

"I heard her murdering her starter motor in your driveway the other day when she dropped by," he joked. "But, no, I haven't seen her."

"Oh. Right."

It was obvious that she would have loved to ask, "What's gone wrong?" but Connor caught the slight shake of John's head that convinced her she shouldn't.

Instead, she asked if he wanted to borrow her

manuscript copy of Nancy Sherlock's book and he halfheartedly agreed. Apart from his hunt for Jerry Purcell, it wasn't as if he had a whole lot else to occupy his free time just lately.

Maybe I'm wrong, he thought, after another fruitless session of calling radio stations the following day. Maybe Jerry has nothing to do with what's going on inside her, and nothing that I can find out about him will help her in any way. Maybe she really isn't looking for a relationship, and she really doesn't think that chemistry counts.

And maybe he'd agree with her if it was only a question of chemistry, but he knew it wasn't. He *knew!* It was so much more than that. So much more. It meant that he couldn't sleep at night, couldn't concentrate on his work. What did it matter what they called the new game? He couldn't stop himself from thinking about her nearly every waking minute, and missing Jane, too—the little baby girl he'd started to hope might one day become his daughter.

He let the weekend slip by. But on Monday, during his lunch break at work, he called his list of radio stations in New York City. On his twelfth call, he hit pay dirt at last.

The receptionist remembered Purcell calling for a job and gave Connor the man's forwarding address. Ten minutes and two phone calls after that, he was sitting with the telephone handset dangling in his fingers and his heart thumping and his mind buzzing with a turn of events that he hadn't expected, that had huge ramifications for Allie, and that he didn't yet have the slightest idea how to deal with.

Rent too high. Stairs too steep. Park too far. Landlord too sleazy.

Is it the Philadelphia rental market? Allie had begun to wonder. *Or is it just me?*

It was lunchtime, and Jane was asleep. Allie was still going through the weekend newspaper, trying to find a place that was both closer to Karen and John, and more suitable for Jane. The search was proving a lot tougher than she'd expected. Maybe she was being too fussy. On the other hand, what was the point of moving at all if she hadn't found a place that fitted?

Jane wouldn't be a baby for too much longer. She would need safety and sunlight and room to move and play. She would need trees and grass and swings and slides near enough to walk to, and Aunt Karen and Uncle John close by so that they could all see each other every week.

And she would need a room big enough for a second bed so that Hope could stay over on the nights before Allie had her program, because the current situation was becoming impossible for all of them.

Maybe there were options Allie was missing. She did feel tired, not always functioning at her best. She rubbed her eyes and tackled the final column of advertisements again. Could she squeak her price ceiling up an extra hundred a month?

The life of a single parent was as physically and

emotionally tough as she'd often heard, and the task of telling her friends about the huge concealed truth in her recent past wasn't something that had come easily to her inner nature. Her friends had been supportive, after the initial shock, but somehow they were shut out of what she was dealing with right now. Despite the radiant blessing of Jane, there were a lot of times over the past couple of weeks when she had felt very alone.

A lot of times? Be honest with yourself, A.J. Todd. Practically all the time. And don't kid yourself. You know why.

It was Connor. She'd never expected, never imagined, such an intense degree of loss and hurt. Anger, too.

How come men never know how to be just friends? How come they always want more, and if a woman hasn't got more to give, they lose interest completely? Did I really need to lose him totally like this?

She hadn't realized, until he was no longer around, how much he'd been there for her as she learned how to be a mother to Jane. And she had to admit, despite her raging anger against him, that there was a way in which a man like Connor really mattered.

Connor had balanced the sweet intensity of her new perceptions as a mother with a salty common sense that was very male, just the way John so often balanced Karen's wilder extravagances of mood and inspiration with his quiet, more grounded wisdom.

Damn you, Connor! I miss you!

The one thing she didn't dare let into her thoughts was the suggestion that he might have been right about the issue that had finally split their tortured relationship in two.

Jerry Purcell.

Don't think about it.

The doorbell of her apartment rang a few minutes later, dragging her away from the final few classifieds she still hadn't checked through. She wasn't expecting anyone, and hauled the door open with the vague assumption that it would be Hope, who had left her library book here ever since last Wednesday, and had forgotten to take it home each day since. It was now a week overdue.

"Connor!" Her voice squeaked through her throat. Automatically, she hugged the sleeves of her lightweight navy sweater.

"Can I come in?" That syrup-on-gravel growl turned her insides to strawberry mousse.

"Of course," she said.

There was something about his attitude that had her dismissing any clever comments or stubbornly worded refusals before they'd even formed in her mind.

"We need to talk," he said. "Where's Jane?"

"Asleep."

"Okay."

He prowled, apparently blind to the details of her small, cozy apartment, which he was seeing for the first time.

"Do you want some coffee?" she asked him.

It was painfully obvious that there was something

on his mind, and her immediate instinct was to help, make it easier for him, whatever it was. Some bad news in his family? She didn't stop to think about why he might turn to her over something like that, or what it meant about the state of her heart that all she wanted was to be there for him.

"Sure." The single syllable was automatic, distracted.

He followed her to the small kitchen and watched her mess with the filter and the coffee grounds. Before she set the coffeemaker going, she had to ask, "What's wrong, Connor?"

His edginess prickled in the air and had her walking on eggshells.

"I don't know how to tell you this," he began.

"You're scaring me."

"I know, I—don't be scared, Allie, but it *is* something major. It's Jerry Purcell."

The sound of the name was like a fist clutching at her throat.

"No! I don't want to—" She shook her head and put her hands over her ears.

"You *have* to." His eyes blazed, but it was sheer emotional intensity more than simple anger. "You have to confront this, Allie." He pulled her hands away from her head. "You'll never be at peace with yourself if you don't. You'll never be able to move on."

"Says the expert," she tried to jeer, but it didn't work, just sounded shaky and weak, which was how she felt.

"I was selfish about it in the beginning," he said.

"For my own sake, for what we could have, I was determined to do something to help you move on. Now, whatever is or isn't going on between us, you just need it for *you*. And after what I learned today…"

"Connor, for mercy's sake, don't keep circling around the subject!" She clasped her hands together, and he nodded, seeming as impatient as she was.

They had both forgotten the coffee, and he was scaring her more by the minute.

"I decided to track him down," he said. "I started contacting radio stations, on the assumption he would have gotten another job in the same area."

"And you did, right?" She leaped ahead of his narrative. "You got hold of him."

"Not quite," he answered her slowly. "I couldn't do that, Allie, as it turned out." His words slowed even further. "You see…he died of a drug overdose in New York City last Saturday night."

"Oh…my…Lord! Oh, my!"

With legs shaking so hard they wouldn't hold her, she sank to the floor and let the news and the memories and the reality wash over her in successive waves. Connor crouched beside her and took her hand, rubbing the way he had her whole body weeks ago up at Diamond Lake to bring the circulation back into her limbs after her fall through the ice. For a long time, neither of them spoke, although she could feel the intensity of his focus like a beam of radiant heat. He was the one who finally broke the silence.

"Can you tell me I was wrong to do it?" His voice cracked. "And wrong to tell you?"

"No, you weren't wrong."

"It was unfinished, wasn't it? You kept telling yourself, and me, that you'd moved on, that it was in the past and had no power over you, didn't you?"

"But I was wrong," she nodded, dazed and sick. She struggled to put it into words. "Jane filled the front of my mind, but lurking in the back of it there was a nightmare that I wasn't admitting to."

"I could sense that."

"That he'd come back into my life somehow. Or maybe not even him, but the effect of what he'd done."

"I know."

"And now he's dead...."

"The funeral is the day after tomorrow."

"Here in Philly?"

"Yes. I've spoken to his family, Allie. His parents. I told them I was the friend of a former colleague of his at WPYR."

"He had a family?" She shook her head, trying to shake the bewilderment away. "Oh, of course he did."

"Yeah, like most people."

"I mean, I knew that. He was an ordinary guy. Not a monster."

"It was a monstrous thing he did."

"It was," she agreed. Now she was the one staring blindly—at his hand, which she was crushing between her sweat-slick palms. Her mind's eye played scenes from the past like a disjointed video clip. "But maybe this is the way to separate the monster from the man. Could that be right? I want to go. To the funeral. Connor, could—" She gripped his arm.

"Of course," he told her, before she even finished asking. "Of course I'm coming with you. That's what I was going to suggest all along."

"Jerry, sadly, had lost his way during the last few years of his life. A lot of us tried to help. None of us could. Trisha turned to us for help for his problems with alcohol and drugs, but Jerry himself couldn't do that. This is one of the things we're all mourning today, as we mourn his loss."

The tenor male voice, which had been steady until now, suddenly cracked and jerked to a halt as Mike Purcell looked down at his parents in the front row of the funeral chapel and couldn't go on with the eulogy he'd prepared.

Way in the background, separated from the immediate family by a good sixty people, Allie sat like a stone, gripping Connor's hand. It hurt, but he didn't care. She hadn't yet introduced herself to the family, but she planned to do so afterward. There were a couple of other people here from WPYR. As another of Jerry's former colleagues, she would blend in. It would be all right.

WPYR's station manager, George Bennett, had actually called Allie the previous afternoon when Connor was still at her apartment, to tell her about Jerry's death. The Purcell family had contacted the station, as they had contacted anyone from Jerry's life that they'd known about. The phone call made Connor doubly glad he'd taken the decision to track Jerry down and therefore heard the news first. It wasn't arrogance on his part to know that the story of Jerry's death had been easier for Allie, coming from him.

Jane was spending the morning with Karen. That had already been planned, and fitted in well with Allie's need to attend the funeral. Karen and John knew what had happened, although Connor sensed that Allie hadn't gone into a lot of detail.

She and Connor had talked for hours yesterday. They had even considered the possibility of telling Jerry's parents that they had another grandchild, but in the end Allie had decided against it, and Connor had supported that decision. Jerry and Trisha had had two kids of their own, it turned out, a boy and a girl aged just one and three, still too young to fully understand what this was all about, too young to fully feel their loss. No one's interests would be served by confronting any of the Purcells with the painful fact of Jane's existence—the living proof of Jerry's weakness—now.

"Okay?" Connor murmured, as the service moved forward again.

"Yes," Allie nodded. "Yes, I am. It's—it was right to come. Even since yesterday, it's made a difference."

Looking at her huge, troubled eyes and petite, rigid body, Connor ached to hold her. Not just her hand, as he was already doing, but her whole body. He wanted to cradle her, kiss away her pain, smooth her hair into place with his fingers, tell her over and over how much he loved her, as if his love alone could strike down everything she was struggling with. But he held back, knowing there was nothing more he could give her right now.

Her courage would have astonished him if he hadn't known her as well as he now did. He thought of the accusations he'd flung at her two weeks ago on the steps of the restaurant. He'd almost called her a coward that night, straight out.

But he could see now that he was wrong. Allie wasn't a coward. She had simply tackled everything that had happened to her over the past seventeen months in her own unique way. Stubbornly. Persistently. Privately. Focusing on one thing at a time.

First, the physical and emotional toll of her pregnancy. Then her battle for life and her battle to accept what she'd then believed to be right—that Jane should belong to Karen. Next, at the point where Connor himself had stepped into the picture, she'd had to deal with her new decision about Jane and what that meant about learning to be a mother. Now, she was facing the final issue, and he wondered how long it would have taken her to do that if he hadn't interfered, and if Jerry hadn't died.

In her own good time, he suspected, she would have dealt with it. When something triggered her need and her readiness. He couldn't kid himself that he'd been a vital part of the process.

He shifted in his seat as a nagging little wind of desolation blew over his spirit. He would have liked to be vital in that way. Now *that* was arrogance!

Connor Callahan, right now you are not even a little black dot in this lady's emotional horizon, he told himself. *You can't blame her for that. There just isn't room inside her for anything as strong as what you feel for her. So accept it and get on with your life, and let her get on with hers.*

Easy to say.

They didn't stay long after the funeral service had concluded, just long enough to say a few words to Jerry's parents and his ex-wife, who all seemed like good-hearted people. As expected, they accepted Allie at face value—a co-worker from WPYR. The fact that Jerry had lost his job at the station through his increasing, secretive drug use was, understandably, not spoken of.

It was a half-hour drive from the funeral home to Connor and Karen and John's street, through neighborhoods where spring was starting to announce its arrival.

Connor had offered the use of his car today, and he was glad Allie had accepted, because she looked exhausted now, very far away inside her own thoughts. She barely spoke, and he didn't push.

Maybe he'd learned his lesson in that department. *A little too late,* he thought, his jaw held so tight that his temples ached. *Much too late.*

Glancing sideways, he saw that she was still hunched like a child with a stomachache, curled up sideways in the passenger seat in her neat, dark gray suit, so that her knees pressed against the car door. It couldn't have been comfortable, but she didn't seem to care.

She only uncurled herself when they turned into his street.

"Going to take some time off?" he asked.

"Not right away," she answered. "My parents are planning a vacation in Arizona next month, and Jane and I will probably share a week of it with them. It's not finalized yet."

"Sounds good."

"It will be," she agreed quietly, then smiled. "I admit, it would be even better if it was tomorrow. But it's not always possible to do your healing when it's most convenient, is it? It has to be scheduled around other commitments, like everything else."

She laughed as she finished, and Connor joined in, but the atmosphere in the car wasn't exactly hilarious, and they both fell silent again until the car's engine purred to a halt in Connor's driveway.

Karen must have been watching for them. She appeared on her front porch at once, with Jane in her arms, and Allie got out of the car and waved before turning back to Connor. She hesitated, as if the words *thank you* weren't powerful enough, but she didn't know any better ones.

He saved her from the awkward moment. "You don't have to say anything," he said. "I'll see you around, okay?"

Then he shoved his car keys into his pocket and went toward his own front steps, gave a wave and quick greeting to Karen, and disappeared inside.

Allie reached Karen and took Jane into her arms just in time to watch Connor unlock his front door and enter the house. There was an aura of finality to the way his door closed after him, like the curtain falling at the end of a play, or the credits beginning to roll after a movie, and she had to hide from Karen the sour surge of disappointment that rode inside her.

Allie spent the rest of the day doing simple things—a little grocery shopping, a little exercise at her gym. Meanwhile, in the back of her mind there was the nagging sense that somewhere in everything that had happened this morning—not so much the funeral, but the time she'd spent with Connor—one of them had said something very significant, something that offered a solution to the problem she couldn't even name. If it wasn't too late....

The only trouble was, she had no idea what the significant words could have been.

Chapter Eleven

Connor scowled and slouched his way through breakfast. He had the radio on, tuned to A.J. Todd's morning drive-time program on Radio WPYR, of course, which felt startlingly similar, emotionally speaking, to head-butting a brick wall.

Since it was drive-time, he ought to be doing just that. But...he wasn't going to do it!

One great thing about Callahan Systems was that the managing directors and owners of the company, i.e. his brothers Patrick and Tom Callahan, had a visionary concept of workplace efficiency when it came to their senior executives. If you couldn't do the job on a Thursday, come in and do it on the weekend instead.

Connor knew that he didn't have a hope of formulating a marketing strategy today. It was all he could do to focus on the strategy of coffee-drinking.

He felt lost, adrift, and he needed answers. Less than twenty-four hours after heroically deciding to let Allie go her own way for as long as it took— which would very probably be forever—he was seething with active rebellion.

I can't do this. Patience is not a Connor Callahan virtue!

Neither was acceptance, self-sacrifice, or passivity. It was...hell, it was maddening, miserable, impossible that the opposite traits of rebellion, self-interest and action had gotten him precisely nowhere.

I love her. I really, really love her. And love is supposed to win. Love isn't supposed to be out of balance, an emotion that one person feels while the other doesn't.

But then, he'd never seen an actual rule book on the subject.

Who was I kidding yesterday? Did I really think something would suddenly change, just because she'd had to confront her past at the funeral?

He felt an urgent, unstoppable craving to *do* something, and the only thing he could think of was to at least *talk*. To Allie's sister, which seemed like the best option, since she was conveniently right next door.

He tipped the rest of his coffee down the sink, charged over to his neighbor's place and was greeted by three things. First, Allie's voice on the radio again. Karen was tuned in to the same station. Second, the sound of Allie's daughter singing in her high chair, not quite as melodious as A.J. Todd and

WPYR's playlist, but close. Third, Karen with a piece of paper in her hand that turned out to be a list of art supplies she needed to pick up. She had a new kids' picture book to illustrate, she was full of second-trimester energy, and Connor only had to take one look at her to feel his impulse for a heart-to-heart ebbing rapidly.

He offered instead to mind Jane. Allie's baby, instead of Allie.

"Would you?" Karen said, tucking an errant strand of light brown hair behind her ear. "She'd probably enjoy that more than shopping. It'll only be for an hour and a half. Allie's coming by right after her program. Am I exploiting you, Connor?"

"Hey, I have nieces," he hedged. "I'm good at this."

He didn't want to admit to the fact that babysitting Allie's daughter brought him closer in spirit to Allie herself, and therefore it was much more probable that *he* was exploiting *her*. Karen hadn't had that matchmaking glint in her eye the past couple of weeks, but it probably wouldn't take much to rekindle it. Another good reason to abandon his hazy idea of a heart-to-heart.

In the almost unnatural silence after she'd gone, he just had time to wonder what had happened to the radio when he realized that it was only the normal hiatus that occurred as a song was dying away. Then Allie's voice came on.

Still sitting up in her high chair, Jane started rocking back and forth excitedly at the sound, and it practically choked him up.

"You love your mom's voice like I do, don't you, Janey?" he said softly. "But unlike me, you don't have to wonder what the heck you're supposed to do about it."

"Call us," A.J. Todd said, as if she could hear him and was offering an answer. "Call, fax, e-mail. We want your requests and we play 'em, here on Philly Country Classic Radio WPYR. All country, all music."

She gave the phone number of the request line, and before Connor had given himself a moment to stop and think, he had gone to the phone on the wall in the big kitchen and dialed it, purely because *somehow* he needed contact with her right now. He was put through to the studio, heard her greeting, and a second later he was on air.

And air was just about the only thing coming out of his mouth, too. Certainly, there was no sound, let alone anything coherent like the name of a song.

"I love your program, A.J." he finally had to say, in a voice that wasn't quite his. "What is it they say? I'm a longtime listener, but a first-time caller."

"Uh-huh," she answered brightly. "We need more of 'em. That means you, Philadelphia."

He was pretty sure she hadn't recognized his voice, and she sounded a little mechanical. Was he reading too much into the fact that she hadn't seemed quite her usual confident self on air this morning? Was she as restless and moody as he was?

"And, uh…" he went on. Not surprising she hadn't recognized him. The frog in his throat was the size of a pregnant buffalo.

"Can we find out who I'm talking to, here?" she said in an encouraging way. She was obviously used to people who dried up on live radio.

"Uh...Connor," he said.

"Connor." She sounded different, suddenly, but as if she still wasn't sure, or wasn't prepared to let it show.

He cursed himself inwardly. Why was he doing this? Just to rattle her in the middle of live broadcasting? Gee, she'd thank him for that. It'd make her swoon right into his arms!

"That's a name I've heard quite a bit of, just lately," she said carefully. "Do you have a request for us this morning, Connor?"

"Uh, yes, I—"

Man! A request! He was on the request line, he was a longtime country-music fan, and every country song he'd ever heard, title and singer, had just flown right out of the gaping window in his brain.

He groped for what felt like minutes and finally came up with, "Uh, how about...'What's In It For Me' by Faith Hill?"

It was a cry from the heart, from the impatient part of him, the part that had to act, not simply sit back and wait, and he wondered if Allie would recognize that, would recognize his voice now. Since she wasn't stupid, she probably would. How would she react?

"Faith Hill. 'What's In It For Me,'" Allie echoed, choking suddenly, as if a hand had come to squeeze her throat. She was in no doubt about who her "first-time caller" was now. "That's...a great track, Connor."

She hugged her arms around herself, drawing no comfort from her cozy ash-gray silk-and-mohair sweater. So he'd decided to ask the big question over the radio? Cute. Unfair, but cute.

While Allie gave a brief rundown of the time and the weather, Charlene cued in the track, the first on Faith Hill's album entitled "Breathe."

Breathe. Yeah, that was a good piece of medical advice, she decided when the first notes sounded.

She took a big gulp of air and sat back, safely off mike for five minutes and thirty-six seconds, and tried to relax her throat.

She hadn't recognized his voice at first. He hadn't sounded all that different from normal—although he had, a little, she decided, thinking back—it was just that his was the last voice she'd expected to hear.

And then that request, with the painful pause and stumbling before it that had made Charlene cross her fingers and get ready to disconnect the line. It sounded as if he had been at a loss for words to start with, and had grabbed the first song that came to mind. But then, as she thought about it, and as the rocking beat and zinging violin blared out, followed by Faith Hill's rich voice belting out the lyrics, she started to hear a deep significance to every line.

"What's In It For Me?"

What *was* in it for him? He'd hung on for a roller-coaster ride that was every bit as rollicking and head-pounding as the glorious, driving rhythm of this music. She'd blown hot and cold, just like the unknown lover Faith Hill was singing to.

Was he giving her one final chance to answer the question? Beyond all the ups and downs, what was in it for him? Did she have the answer he wanted?

Music had always been a powerful emotional trigger for Allie, and today it was no different. At first she had to fight back tears and then, all of a sudden, came revelation.

What had she said to him yesterday? She had been talking about the planned vacation with her parents in Arizona. Something about a person not always being able to do their healing when it was convenient.

That's what I've been trying to do, she realized. *Get my healing done and out of the way, clear the in-tray on my emotional desk before I started to think about the possibility of getting involved. And that's wrong. Sometimes life doesn't give us the luxury of convenient timing. If I want him...if I love him...oh, and I do, I love him with all my soul...I have to take the love from him. Only I didn't understand that until now.*

Now, as the song ended, and she had to jump in with her bright, sexy, on-air voice and talk to her disembodied listeners about what was up next and what giveaways they had.

Giveaways? Forget giveaways!

"Thanks for that, Connor," she said instead.

She could see him in her mind's eye as she spoke. Could see his sensitive mouth ready to kiss her, and spread wide in a white-toothed grin. Could see his eyes like dark pools at night, and sparkling blue in the snow at Diamond Lake. Could see the silly faces he made for Jane, and the square-jawed look he got when he was talking guy talk with John or one of his brothers.

"I've loved that song since I first heard it," she went on. "But...for some reason, I heard even more in its lyrics today. How about we play another track from the 'Breathe' album? It's another one of my favorites. 'That's How Love Moves.' Philadelphia, you're tuned to WPYR."

When the song finished, she said, "Thanks for choosing something from that album, Connor. There are some beautiful songs on it. And I have a feeling those two in particular may end up meaning a lot to me...one way or the other."

"Allie, hell, why do you sound like that?" Connor muttered under his breath. "That's not how I want you to sound."

She was choking, shaky, as if she was about to cry. The flirty, sexy quality, which usually made it sound as if she was sharing a wicked private joke with every one of her listeners, had gone.

A.J. on the radio wasn't going to answer him. The only person who could do that was Allie live in front of him, flesh and blood.

He was too impatient to wait until she finished her program and drove back here. He was even half-afraid she would be too upset to come home. He unstrapped Jane from her high chair, grabbed her diaper bag from the hall table and trusted—in spite

of Allie's unfortunate experience a few weeks ago—
that there would already be diapers in it.

Then he headed for his car.

Was just about to lock Karen's front door behind
him—and he had no key—when he remembered that
he didn't have a car seat. Cursed for a moment.
Thought laterally.

Jane was sitting up in a toddler seat now, but she
must have had an infant seat until a couple of
months ago. Yes, that was what she'd been in at
Diamond Lake. Maybe it was still around. And she
couldn't have grown that much. She'd still squeeze
into it. He checked the basement and found it immediately.

Was that the only piece of good luck he would
get today? He hardly had the patience to find out.
He drove through weather that was turning nastier
by the minute—the falling snow was starting to settle on the cold cement of the sidewalks—and parked
outside WPYR at exactly three minutes after Allie
came off air.

Letting herself out of the studio building and pulling her dark coat collar up, Allie saw Connor before
he saw her. She felt hope and relief crash over her
like a wave, and her heart seemed to jump into her
throat. Both body parts were getting an intensive
workout today.

He was holding Jane, and busy pulling her woolly
hat up from her eyes and zipping her little yellow
and mauve down jacket. Snow had already started

to feather their clothing, white lace on the black background of Connor's coat.

What were the two of them doing here? As far as Allie knew, Connor was supposed to be at work—she had assumed earlier that he was calling her request line from his office—and Jane was supposed to be with Karen at home. Seeing them like this made her incredibly nervous, after the exchange of meaningful song titles that she hadn't known if she was interpreting right. It was as if the snowflakes all around were whirling in her stomach as well.

Now he had seen her. He didn't come any closer, just stood by the car, waiting and watching as she approached, his face serious and his expressive mouth straight and closed. Allie was jittery and aching with the effort of reining in her throbbing nerves, of staying enough in control to keep walking toward him.

When she got close enough they said, "Hi," to each other in a shy sort of way, like teenagers.

Jane wasn't so tentative. She beamed at both of them and stretched her arms out to Allie. The sleeves of her jacket were too long. Just the pink tips of her longest three fingers were visible on each hand.

"What...did we just say to each other back there, Connor?" Allie asked, trying to smile as if it was a joke, although they both knew it wasn't. "I wasn't...quite sure in the end."

"Yeah. Me, too. That's why I came—to get a little clarification on the subject," he agreed, just as carefully. "Your voice on the radio... The words of that second song..."

"No, you tell me about the one you asked for first..." Her breathing was shallower than ever.

"Allie, I didn't plan it," he answered in a rush. "It just happened. I was at Karen's, looking after Jane for a little while. I called your request line on an impulse, and then that song came into my head. And it fit so well. All the ups and downs."

"So well," she agreed. "It was scary! How could I not answer with a song of my own?"

"I heard it."

"Then I started to wonder. 'What's In It For Me.' Maybe that was a kiss-off, not a cry from the heart."

"Allie, believe me, it was a cry from the heart. But I could tell you weren't sure. I came straight over, so we could say it face-to-face. Actually, so I could make quite certain you *wanted* to say it face-to-face. Seems like maybe you do, darlin'."

"Oh, Connor..."

He reached out for her, just as Jane was doing, and the three of them held each other, with the snow falling on them like a benediction.

"Allie, I love you," he said urgently. He pressed his mouth on hers, over and over, between every phrase. "I've told you that before. You've thrown it back in my face. More than once."

She sagged against him, feeling her strength drain away and her body melt into his.

"But the way your voice sounded on the ra-dio—" he went on.

"Yeah, my producer wasn't too thrilled," she

agreed, bowing her head and feeling him press kisses into her hair. "Not my best day."

"*I'm* thrilled," he said. "Because all I can think is that it means you have to care. Am I right? Tell me you do." He curled his fingers under her chin and coaxed her head up so he could see her expression. "Tell me you're ready now. What's in this for me, Allie?"

"Everything you want…everything I can give," she whispered, so low that he had to nuzzle his cheek to hers in order to hear. "And it seems like things are changing inside me so fast, I have more to give you every day."

She didn't speak any more for a long moment, didn't try to explain, just buried her face in the shoulder of his coat, then stretched out her hands to pull his face close to hers.

And he didn't seem to need an explanation. Not yet. His mouth moved hungrily on hers, tasting her triumphantly, exuberantly, with a possessive eagerness that sent her senses spinning into overdrive. A snowflake landed on her eyelash and he licked it off with the tip of his tongue. Another one landed on the corner of his mouth and she kissed it away, feeling the tiny, icy tingle of melting water on her lips.

Finally, he ordered, "Talk, Allie, before Jane gets sick of this. I want to hear it *all* now."

"I love you. I love you, Connor."

"I know. Ah, Allie, I know you do, and it feels so good to hear you say it. Why couldn't you say it before? Why couldn't you feel it? Was I right? Was it Jerry?"

"Kind of," she agreed. Frowning, she traced a finger over his cold face, mapping the features she loved. "Not as simple as that, though."

"Tell me," he urged. He captured her finger in his mouth, gave it a teasing lick, then repeated, "You have to tell me so I can understand. We need to get on some solid ground, here."

"It just seemed like I was overwhelmed. Like—" She sighed and struggled for the words. "This is the way I thought of it just now. It's not a great metaphor, but... It was like my emotional in-tray was overflowing, with so much important stuff in it that there just wasn't room for you as well. Felt like I had to clear it first."

"No, it *is* great. It's a good metaphor," he told her.

"Then I said to you yesterday," she went on, "that healing couldn't always be slotted into the timetable of a person's life when it was most convenient. All night that nagged at me. Only I couldn't see how it was significant—until this morning when you called on the radio and I realized. To hell with timing! You're in my life *now,* we've fallen in love *now,* totally in love, and I just have to slot that into the equation."

"You mean the in-tray?"

"The whatever." She waved her hand. "And deal with it right *now.* Does that make any sense to you at all?" She captured his face between her palms and searched his expression. Jane did an exploration of her own, grabbing at his ear.

"Allie," he answered, "it makes so much sense

that I don't know why I couldn't have thought of it that way myself, oh, about four weeks ago. I could have convinced you of it and saved us both a whole lot of doubt and pain.''

"Don't talk about it that way," she said. "That's another thing I've had to tell myself these past couple of months, whenever I've thought about the time with Jane that I lost. It happened the way it had to happen. That's all. Simple. There's no sense in any regret. I don't want to dwell on the negative anymore, Connor.''

"I know. It's the same for me. There is no negative right now. There's only you, and Jane, and everything we're going to have together.''

"It won't always be that way. There may still be problems...." She trailed off.

"Sure, there may be problems," he agreed, wrapping his arms more tightly around her. His blue eyes blazed with confidence now, catching her up in their jeweled light. "Everyone has problems. When they come, we'll deal with them together. Isn't that what we've done from the beginning? We dealt with Karen getting stuck in the storm and leaving you with Jane. We dealt with you falling through the ice, and realizing that you wanted to be Jane's mom. Today, I'm not thinking about problems, okay? In fact, they're the last thing on my mind.''

"What *are* you thinking about, Connor Callahan?" She smiled. She felt as if she'd just stepped into a whole new world.

"Um, Brady and Savannah, actually," he said.

There was a new glint in his eye, and a seductive lilt to his voice.

"Brady and…?"

"Nancy's book. Karen lent me the manuscript last week, and I read it on the weekend."

"I know who they are, I'm just wondering how—"

"We're standing here in the snow, just the way Brady and Savannah were on Karen's cover. And I'm thinking that we owe quite a lot to those two strong-minded characters. And to baby Will," he added, squeezing Jane's shoulders.

"I guess we do…."

Jane squealed. For whatever reason, she seemed to be loving this. She was looking back and forth between the two of them, as they held each other, smiling as if her face might split.

"Do you remember what Karen told us about how the book ended?" Connor asked.

"Remind me," Allie whispered, although it had come back to her in a flash. A hot, hot flash.

"Well, they'd tended to the dying sheriff and he'd married them in his last minutes of life."

"Married them, huh?" she echoed. "I guess he did."

"Gotta end with a wedding, Allie."

"Sounds good to me," she murmured, her lips soft and seductive against his mouth.

"Is that a yes?"

"Yes. Very definitely a yes."

"Can we live in my house? There's room for, oh, at least three kids."

"I love your house...."

"But *after* their wedding," he went on, after a considerable pause, "when the deputy had come to take the sheriff away, through the falling snow..."

"And Brady and Savannah found themselves alone at last," Allie came in softly.

"They'd been burning for each other for so long, they barely made it back into the cabin. The fire was blazing. Baby Will was asleep in his little wooden cradle. They pulled off each other's snow-soaked clothes and left a trail of them from the front door through to Brady's bed. And then. Ah, then, Allie..."

"And then," she pointed out, "don't you remember? They just closed the bedroom door."

"I know," he agreed, grinning. "They closed the bedroom door. Best moment in the whole book. The power of the imagination is a wonderful thing. And all I want to know right now is—"

"You can close my bedroom door anytime you like, Connor Callahan," Allie whispered, anticipating his question. "Any time at all."

"That's exactly the answer I was hoping for."

* * * * *

If you enjoyed what you just read,
then we've got an offer you can't resist!

Take 2 bestselling love stories FREE!

Plus get a FREE surprise gift!

You're not going to believe this offer!

In October and November 2000, buy any two Harlequin or Silhouette books and save $10.00 off future purchases, or buy any three and save $20.00 off future purchases!

Just fill out this form and attach 2 proofs of purchase (cash register receipts) from October and November 2000 books and Harlequin will send you a coupon booklet worth a total savings of $10.00 off future purchases of Harlequin and Silhouette books in 2001. Send us 3 proofs of purchase and we will send you a coupon booklet worth a total savings of $20.00 off future purchases.

Saving money has never been this easy.

I accept your offer! Please send me a coupon booklet:

Name: _____

Address: _____ City: _____

State/Prov.: _____ Zip/Postal Code: _____

Optional Survey!

In a typical month, how many Harlequin or Silhouette books would you buy new at retail stores?

☐ Less than 1   ☐ 1   ☐ 2   ☐ 3 to 4   ☐ 5+

Which of the following statements best describes how you buy Harlequin or Silhouette books? Choose one answer only that best describes you.

☐ I am a regular buyer and reader
☐ I am a regular reader but buy only occasionally
☐ I only buy and read for specific times of the year, e.g. vacations
☐ I subscribe through Reader Service but also buy at retail stores
☐ I mainly borrow and buy only occasionally
☐ I am an occasional buyer and reader

Which of the following statements best describes how you choose the Harlequin and Silhouette series books you buy new at retail stores? By "series," we mean books within a particular line, such as *Harlequin PRESENTS* or *Silhouette SPECIAL EDITION*. Choose one answer only that best describes you.

☐ I only buy books from my favorite series
☐ I generally buy books from my favorite series but also buy books from other series on occasion
☐ I buy some books from my favorite series but also buy from many other series regularly
☐ I buy all types of books depending on my mood and what I find interesting and have no favorite series

Please send this form, along with your cash register receipts as proofs of purchase, to:
In the U.S.: Harlequin Books, P.O. Box 9057, Buffalo, NY 14269
In Canada: Harlequin Books, P.O. Box 622, Fort Erie, Ontario L2A 5X3

(Allow 4-6 weeks for delivery) Offer expires December 31, 2000.   PHQ4002

SILHOUETTE *Romance*

COMING NEXT MONTH

#1480 HER HONOR-BOUND LAWMAN—Karen Rose Smith
Storkville, USA
He was tall, dark and older, and he took her in when she'd had no home...or identity. When Emma Douglas's memory returned, she believed she and Sheriff Tucker Malone could have a future. But would the honor-bound lawman she'd come to love accept her in his bed...and in his heart?

#1481 RAFFLING RYAN—Kasey Michaels
The Chandlers Request...
"Sold for $2,000!" With those words wealthy Ryan Chandler reluctantly became earthy Janna Monroe's "date" for a day. Though bachelors for auction seemed ludicrous to Ryan, even crazier was his sudden desire to ditch singlehood for this single mom!

#1482 THE MILLIONAIRE'S WAITRESS WIFE—Carolyn Zane
The Brubaker Brides
For heiress turned waitress Elizabeth Derovencourt, money equaled misery. But her family, not their fortune, mattered. So she visited her ailing grandmother...with a dirt-poor denim-clad cowboy in tow as her "husband." Only she hadn't banked on Dakota Brubaker's irresistible charm—or his millions!

#1483 THE DOCTOR'S MEDICINE WOMAN—Donna Clayton
Single Doctor Dads
Dr. Travis Westcott wanted to adopt twin Native American boys, which was why he welcomed medicine woman Diana Chapman into his home. But somehow the once-burned beauty made Travis want to propose *another* addition to his family: a wife!

#1484 THE THIRD KISS—Leanna Wilson
The first kiss was purely attraction. Brooke Watson and Matt Cutter didn't believe in lasting love. But everyone else did, particularly their nagging families, which was why Brooke agreed to playact the tycoon's beaming bride-to-be. Yet as a *real* wedding date loomed, was a happily-ever-after possible?

#1485 THE WEDDING LULLABY—Melissa McClone
Their marriage had lasted only one night. No problems, no heartache. But unexpectedly Laurel Worthington found herself expecting! When she told father-to-be Brett Matthews her news, he insisted they marry again. But Laurel wasn't about to settle for anything but the *real* golden ring....

CMN1000